WHALE EYES

A MEMOIR ABOUT SEEING AND BEING SEEN

by James Robinson

illustrated by Brian Rea

PENGUIN WORKSHOP

PENGUIN WORKSHOP
An imprint of Penguin Random House LLC
1745 Broadway, New York, New York 10019

First published in the United States of America by Penguin Workshop,
an imprint of Penguin Random House LLC, 2025

Text copyright © 2025 by James Alden Robinson
Illustrations copyright © 2025 by Brian Rea

PENGUIN is a registered trademark and PENGUIN WORKSHOP
is a trademark of Penguin Books Ltd, and the W colophon is a registered trademark
of Penguin Random House LLC.

Visit us online at penguinrandomhouse.com.

Library of Congress Cataloging-in-Publication Data is available.

Manufactured in China

ISBN 9780593523957   10 9 8 7 6 5 4 3 2 1 TOPL

The text is set in Albertina MT Pro.
The handwriting text is set in Kristina, a font made from Brian Rea's handwriting.
The illustrations were drawn with a graphite pencil on paper and then color was digitally applied.

Design by James Robinson and Mary Claire Cruz

This is a work of nonfiction.
Some names and identifying details have been changed.

For Mom

MY EYES

YOUR EYES

Stare intensely at the white dot in the center of the image

for 30 seconds and then flip to page 2.

Afterimage

1   2   3   4   When you stare into the white dot at the center of this portrait   5   6   7   8   and hold your gaze for thirty seconds   9   10   11   your brain begins to play tricks on you.   12   13   14   15   16   17   18. As you allow the surrounding images to fade and blur   19   20   21   22   the cells in your retina get tired. 23   24   25   They've been stimulated for so long that they can no longer send signals to your brain with the same strength.   26   27   So that when you turn the page   28   29   as your mental clock strikes   30 . . .

. . . and stare into an empty canvas,
your world inverts.

Cold blues become warm yellows. Flashy reds fade to gentle greens. The neon scream of an image suited for an electro-punk album cover now smiles back at you with an ever-fading stare that is soft and floating. It hovers in your visual field before fading like a Polaroid in reverse.

Your eyes have just lied to you.

They sent a signal to your brain of an image that didn't actually exist. And for a few moments, the neon screech of fluorescent art turned into a face that was recognizable. A boy. A baby. Held in his parents' arms, smiling from beneath the brim of his sun hat.

But outside of the coloration from your tired retinas and confused brain, the image never existed on the page.

Memory

Memory is a lot like afterimage. It's fleeting and meandering, transforming as you do. Its colors fade and tickle your brain. And it's elusive. You stretch out your hands to grab it and find yourself grasping the air.

If you could take a camera into your brain and record a video of what your memories look like, I think they would resemble the texture and aura of an afterimage.

Sharp edges blur: Desks have lost their drawers and faces their wrinkles. Closets become dressers, and dressers turn to windows.

Backdrops can be hard to decipher. Front yards become backyards become playgrounds.

I used to think that memory's fickleness was its weakness. Why would I put my trust in something that lies, bends, cuts, and is never quite so?

But I've come to learn that there is power in memory's flexibility. Memory, just like afterimage, is capable of inverting. Memories that are hot and flashy with the fires of anger can become cool sources of comfort and belonging. In moments when we once felt isolation and difference, we can look back and sense community.

Sometimes our memories invert because of things we cannot control. A loved one passes, and a memory of laughter can turn into tears or tears into laughter. Granddad's constant muttering of "whatever," a response that once sparked frustration, now brings a smile wrapped in the comfort that he wasn't willing to get caught up in day-to-day conflict.

Other times, when we stare into our memories with focus and curiosity, we unexpectedly ignite this inversion.

That Was Me

The image that just evaporated from the page was of me in 1997 when I was one year old. It was taken during a time when I would laugh, endlessly, often without reason.

When family friends would shout from across the lawn, "How big is Jamo?" my hands would shoot up above my head as they chanted the words that I couldn't yet say: "Jamo is sooooooooooo big."

The memories that I hold from that time come from other people's words, eyes, and photographs. I am told I was once found sitting in front of the fridge with a spoon in one hand and a tub of butter in the other. In the months

that followed, when I crawled out of sight, my parents would go searching for "butter boy."

But it was at this time—when I was spooning for butter, tossing my hands in the air, and giggling from the confines of my stroller—that something critical was occurring within my brain. Through my eyes, I saw a world that was multiplying and doubling and hard to comprehend.

To make sense of it all, my brain was learning to negotiate with my eyes. The resolution that they came to during those first two years would set my life on a course of difference. And indifference.

It would leave me with a set of memories that I never really wished were attached to me. Things I wanted to keep hidden or buried in a dresser whose number of drawers I can't quite remember. Memories that I needed to unwrap carefully, sitting and stirring with them, until the moment when they caught me by surprise and inverted my world.

There are few things worse

than getting in trouble.

One of those

things is reading.

Dear Time

It's Tuesday at ten a.m.

Pencils down.

It's time to practice lying.

But first, you'll have to do some digging.

You lift the lid of your desk and rest it on the top of your head. In goes the Spider-Man eraser. It's time to find the book that Mrs. Surface gave to you last week. She was excited that it would be a "challenge book."

Searching for it requires a deep desk dive, but you are bound to hear it, because it's a library book—meaning it crinkles. That glossy cellophane that they put over hardcovers—the one that makes every new book look old—always announces its presence. It also collects the fingerprints and splotches of every first grader who has ever checked it out. Now it's your turn to add to the collage.

When D.E.A.R. indoctrination began last September, you didn't mind the alone time. At assembly, they had made it sound abrupt and interesting, almost naughty.

Drop
Everything
And
Read

The same teachers who drew a star on the board next to your name when you helped out by picking up a classmate's dropped pencil—and would erase one if you had slammed the kneeling benches in chapel—were now encouraging you to drop all of your belongings out of a sudden enthusiasm for reading.

Back in September, you were allowed to pick any book off the shelf—like *Bats!* or *Nobody Listens to Andrew*. These books were friendly. Their meaning could be derived as much from the illustrations as the words on the page, so nobody would notice if you spent a half hour admiring the art, like a guest in a museum.

But by late March, you weren't allowed to look at

those books during D.E.A.R. And at best, the new ones
would have one illustration per chapter.

It left you in a tough spot. You hated getting in
trouble. But not nearly as much as you hated reading.

D.E.A.R.

Each time I gazed upon the acronym written on the
whiteboard, I imagined the puzzle of a doe and fawn at
my grandmother's house. The acronym didn't make much
sense, partly because spelling wasn't my forte. Wouldn't
it have been easier just to write "R.E.A.D.," which is the
same four letters yet provides far more accurate imagery?

And while we're at it, why not give other subjects
an acronym that has barely any relation to the activity?
Should we call gym Running Around With Rhythm?
What about snack time: Sit At Table And Nibble?
Perhaps at a Catholic school, the acronym wouldn't be
appreciated.

Finally, you hear the crinkle. It's coming from
underneath your math workbook. Rummaging complete,
you yank it out. The room feels silent. You quietly lower
your desk lid and peer over the top. You're last. Again.

Heads on elbows. Chins on fists. Backs slouched against butterfly cushions. Everyone is reading. How did they get there so fast?

Mrs. Surface is hovering beside you. "Are you ready to get started?" she whispers.

Mrs. Surface always felt more like a friend than a teacher. She had been over to your house, and you to hers. She was always there to catch you when you were about to fall. Most of the time, metaphorically.

"What page are you on?" Mrs. Surface whispers.

"Thirty-two," you whisper back, unfurling the book and opening it to a random page somewhere near the front.

Everyone Else Is Reading

You gaze into your book, allowing your eyes to blur, and you begin doing all the things that look like reading but aren't actually reading.

Head held still, your eyes wander off the page and slink across the floor. You see Logan twitching his foot, his untied shoelace just barely grazing the ground.

Beyond the desk legs, a bookmark has fallen. Probably Caroline's. The good-behavior paper chain behind her has almost reached the top of the purple plastic bucket, and is now three or maybe even two links away from the pizza party.

Zach is breathing loudly next to you. He is totally absorbed in his book.

Have you ever watched someone read? Their eyeballs jitter across the page. It's not smooth like sledding. It actually looks more like hopscotch. Sudden abrupt jumps, both eyes exactly matching.

There's a lump under your page, and you realize it's a sunken bookmark—just a few pages ahead. You jump to that page. At least your bookmark knows where you are. Or where you last gave up.

Clocking In

The key to speeding up the clock during D.E.A.R. is to allow your mind to get lost in a story so rambunctious or a memory so vivid that you forget you're stuck in a classroom, imprisoned by the silence of your peers' productivity.

It's time to let your mind meander. You stare at the tennis balls that have an X sliced in them. Mrs. Surface jammed them onto the end of each chair leg so that your class could slide and glide rather than screech.

Nothing.

Ticking.

A sigh.

Getting your mind going is a lot like watching Dad start his old green Saab on the way to school. It takes a few tries. And the more you let your frustration build, the longer it seems to take for the car to get started.

Back to the classroom.

Daniel is turning the page of his spy novel.

Hayley's reading about horses.

Mrs. Surface glances up from her desk. Better turn a page.

You think about recess. At ten fifteen, you will line up at the door and start a chant. The whole class will pump their arms back and forth, cheering "L-E-T-S G-O, Let's Go, Let's Go. L-E-T-S G-O, LETTTTSSSSZZZZ GO!!!"

You chant twice in your head. But then it fades to silence.

Nothing.

Dear Time, please go faster.

You're still stuck in the room.

You flip another page. Page flipping is key. Spend too much time on a page, and you might catch the teacher's attention. She might come over and ask you how the book is going or—worse yet—quiz your comprehension.

It's tempting to move your head and stare at the ceiling and walls for inspiration. But to avoid suspicion, you have to keep your head tilted down and pointed toward the book. This severely limits the amount of exploration that your eyes can do.

You look for the teacher's assistant, who usually sits by the door. She gives you winks throughout the day. And sometimes candy. But she's not there.

You sneak a glance at Mrs. Surface's big beige desk. And remember a week earlier, when you crouched behind it and wiggled on a pair of blue jeans for the school play.

You were a sunflower in a dyed, mud-color shirt, wearing a yellow hat with a crown of felt petals. Your neighbors, the Shears, had shown up to the dress rehearsal to watch you perform. They were the only ones in attendance.

The performance, which lasted the length of a single song, began with you crouched in a ball, head resting against the wood floor with your eyes closed tight. You were a seed. There was a part in the music when the entire class was supposed to sprout up together. The teacher asked if everyone heard the moment when the cymbals clashed. Everyone nodded. You had no idea, but nodding was the easiest option.

You think you hear a light cymbal crash and begin to sprout—popping your head up from your knees with a big smile. And then you glance to the side to see two rows of your classmates still curled up as seeds.

Too early. Back down you go. The rare case of a plant un-sprouting.

You try to listen for cymbals, or clashes, or a fourth beat. Perhaps counting will help. Then you hear someone whisper your name: a whisper from the front row as Mrs. Shears notices a missing plant.

You are still able to peek out at the last minute—when spring is almost over. The last one to grow.

Of course, the Shears still clapped like you gave the best performance. And perhaps it was the most entertaining.

Eight minutes have passed. You got lucky with your classroom seat this month. It faces the clock so you don't have to contort your body to peek at the time. Better turn the page.

You allow your mind to twist and wander.

And then, seventeen minutes in, you feel a kick on your shin.

It came from one of the desks in your quad, either Forest or Charlie.

It probably wasn't Charlie. He's not a kicker.

You flip the page, a subtle way of announcing, *Hey, I'm reading here.*

Even though it hasn't been a full two minutes since your last page flip, it has been a while since you gave yourself a short interval. Short pages are your favorite. Sometimes you even read them.

Then, another kick.

It is Forest. Now you're intrigued.

"James . . . ," he whispers.

You ignore him, not wanting to get into trouble.

Again, this time louder, "James . . ."

You look up. "What?"

A few classmates peek up from their books. You stare back at him. But he's not relenting.

"James, your book."

The kerfuffle has raised eyebrows. Mrs. Surface is walking toward the desk now.

"Is something the matter, boys?" Mrs. Surface asks as she hovers over your shoulder.

"Umm, Mrs. Surface," Forest announces, his subtle upspeak suggesting he is about to tattle. "James's book is upside down."

It's an abrupt revelation. And you have little time for recovery, since Mrs. Surface is already standing right next to you.

You bring the page into focus. He's not wrong. The words are upside down.

But the real problem is bigger than that. Not only have you been holding it upside down, but with each carefully timed flip of the page, you have been going backward, closer and closer to the beginning of the book. You told Mrs. Surface that you were starting on page thirty-two. Now you are on seventeen.

Neither the page number nor the whispers and giggles spreading throughout the classroom seem to matter to Mrs. Surface.

Instead, she crouches down to eye level and catches you in your lie with one simple question: "What happened in your book today?"

Shall We Flip?

I've always felt that the act of reading a book upside down was underappreciated.

So let's give it a go.

Turn to page 37 and invert the book.

and you realize you've
been holding your book
upside down?

And that even though

you started on page 37,

Now you're on 22

and need to catch up,
so turn to page 38.

What are you going to do when someone calls out your name

Or what about your favorite part?

Or if you recommend it?

when someone asks you if you like this book?

What are you going to say

towel out over the sink

This is what it feels like to be taken hostage by a book. To be there to it, yet un-able to interact.

To be grasping its edge, but never r its meaning.

What   w   ou   l   d

                    it   be   like

to   make it   to   the   bottom

of   the   page?

To be   one   of   the   who

never   ha   dan   pe o p le   is   sue

        w   i   t   h   r   e   a   d   i   ng?

To   never hav   e   to   the

words   f   i   g   h   t

or   co   m   p   e   l   them   into focus?

To   for   ce   out   their

mean   ings   like   wringing

    w   r   i n   ging   a

The key here is to get your mind racing down a track so distant that it doesn't come back to where you are. Find a way to start speeding it up. It's like taking your imagination for a jog. You need to find a way for the time to pass. Three minutes.

Look up at the clock. How long has it been?

up

h

I fe ls li   t e wor   he
                        av gi   on   u.
                          ʌ

                                    o
        e
              ə
ɾ   ʞ
                                u

            d   y
        s

    ǝ

Sometimes

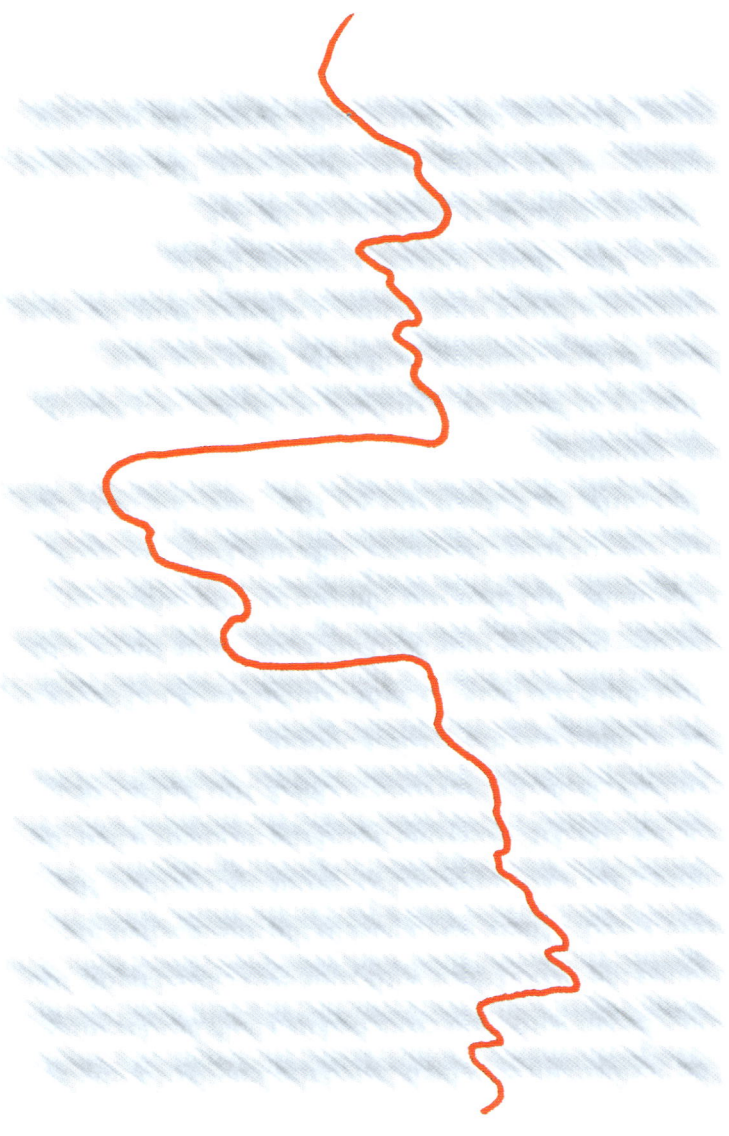

Finding avalanches and rivers

in the shapes they make.

Sometimes I like to focus on the space
between the letters.

Rock

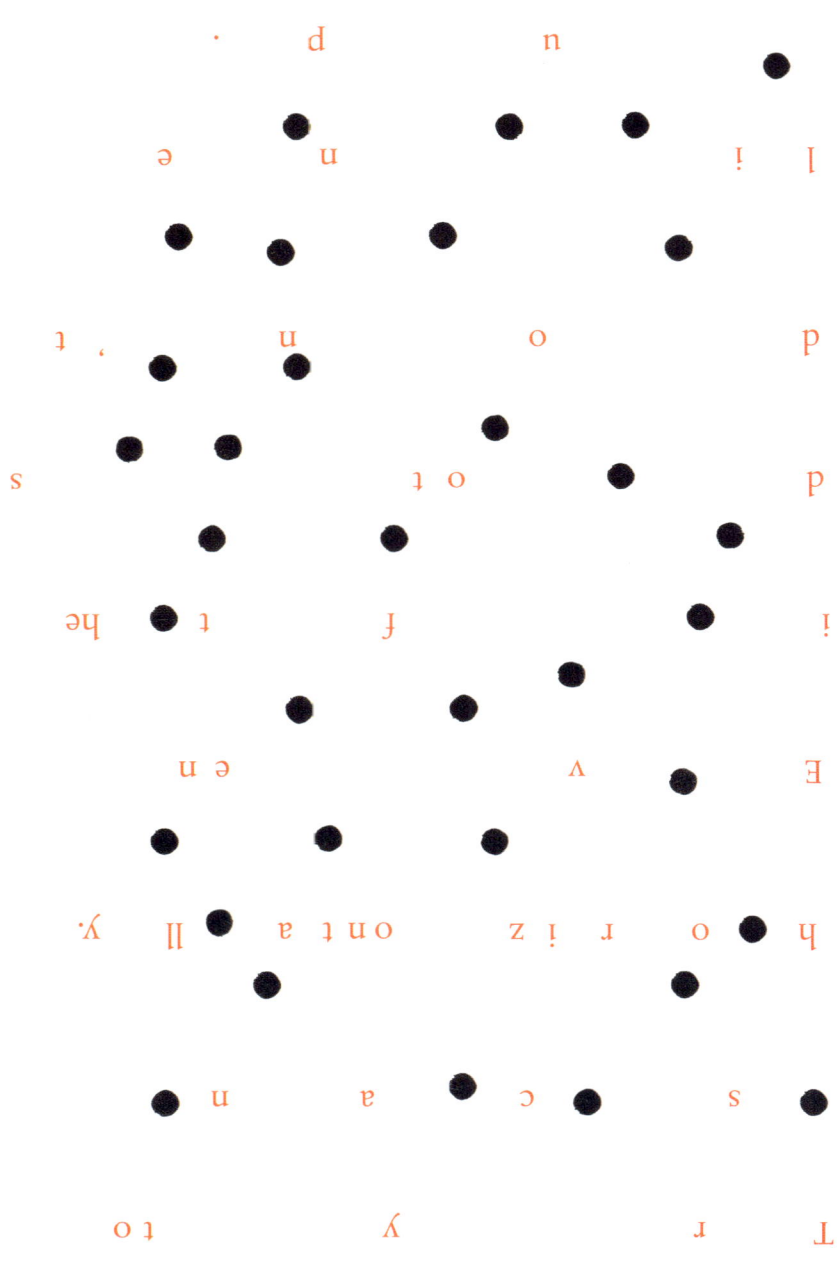

It will look like you're reading if you pick random spots on the page and hold your gaze ● for different amounts of time.

For added effect, you can lick your finger
before turning the page.

It will look like you're reading.

It looks like you're reading if you place your pointer finger in the middle of the page and slowly guide it down one line at a time.

listening to the sound of the room around you. In film, they call this room tone. The sounds that a room makes with no other source of noise.

The low buzz of an air conditioner.

Or the gradual ticking of an old radiator—the one that you can strum your pencil across while walking by as if playing a xylophone.

Listen to the tone of the fan. The buzz of lights. The swoosh of cars passing by. Is there a steady beat? A constant hum? Does it fade in and out?

You may be wondering if it is time to turn the page.

Not quite yet.

We need to start pretending.

Allow your eyes to fly back and forth. To snake across the page. Try following these lines:

Let's Begin

Put yourself in a public place.

Maybe a library.

Or a couch.

Or a park bench, where a human being may

notice you.

What is it like to be holding the book upside down?

What do you feel?

Shame?

Excitement?

Thrill?!

Nothing?

Okay, I'm going to teach you how to pretend-read.

Are you comfy? Eyes aimed at the page? Begin by

Right Side Up Again

When I sat in my chair, face-to-face with Mrs. Surface,
pretending that I hadn't just gone a full twenty-three
minutes reading my book upside down, I didn't feel guilty.
Because I wasn't lying any more than I had been lied to.

Reading, itself, felt like a great big lie. I had been
promised an adventure to a far-off land. I had been
intrigued by the librarian who captured our attention
with a mystery, enticing us to predict the ending before
she finished reading us the book.

But when I tried it alone, the words had betrayed me.
The longer I stared at each page, the more I felt an aching
in my head and behind my eyes. When I flipped to the next
page, the afterimage of the previous page floated in my
field of vision, reminding me how long I had been staring.

The more tired I became, the more the words appeared to jump in and out of view.

Just finding my way on the page was an activity that took effort. And frequently as I proceeded forward, I would find myself reading the same line of text twice in would find myself reading the same line of text twice in a row, not realizing until midway through that I had made a mistake and would need to start the sentence over again.

The page and the words on it became an obstacle course, and it sometimes seemed that it required just as much energy to navigate the obstacles as it did to derive meaning from the words on the page.

Staring at these splotches of ink and watching them blur, it seemed impossible that I would ever be able to find meaning, emotion, story, character, suspense, and all the little things that were supposed to make reading enjoyable.

Instead, I would be left wondering if there would ever be a time when I would make it to the end of a book. When the weight in my left hand would be more than the weight in my right. When I wouldn't feel the need to zoom ahead and count how many pages were left until the chapter was over. I wondered if there would ever be a time when Mrs. Surface could ask me what my book was about, and I could look her in the eye and give her a real answer.

I watched classmates take flight, shifting in their seats, tapping their feet, and flipping the pages with vigor and excitement. I was alone. Not the alone where you're by yourself. But instead, that piercing and stranded kind of alone. When you're surrounded by people who have abandoned you, even though they're still within arm's reach.

But even if I couldn't keep up with my classmates, I could at least mimic their physical being as they took flight. I could sink into a scholarly slouch. And rest my head on my hand, and my elbow on the edge of the desk. I could flip the pages with such vigor and excitement that it would sound like there was no place else I would rather be than here. With you. Reading.

My Mistake

There was one critical mistake that I made with my lying. It's a mistake that I repeated in middle school, when I groaned my way through Seamus Heaney's translation of *Beowulf* and spent twenty minutes decoding the meaning of two lines, which amounted to nothing more than "the sun rose."

It's a mistake I still sometimes make while reading the narrow columns of the *New Yorker* magazine when I have to remind myself I don't hate the story but the thinness of the columns that jump out of view.

I had failed to differentiate between the words on the page and the container that was carrying them.

I didn't just lose faith in the power of reading but in the words themselves. If there was one thing that was going to get me out of the hole I was digging for myself, it would be words. I just needed to find a way to come to peace with them. On my own terms.

The Red Dot

It's time for a test.

Rotate your book so that this text is right side up,

and then flip to the next page to begin.

Is the red dot **inside** or **outside** the white box?

Is the red dot inside **or outside** the white box?

One more time.

Inside?   Outside?

The thing that's so frustrating about the red dot test is that everyone else in line at the first-grade vision and hearing test seems to do it so seamlessly.

As you wait anxiously for your turn, you hear a smattering of responses.

"inside"

"outside"

"inside"

"in side"

"out side"

No hesitation. Never a moment of confusion. No one looks up from the eyepiece to check if the nurse has started the experiment yet, or if the machine that you stare into each fall is malfunctioning.

And yet when it is your turn to step up and press your forehead against the rubber pad so that you can stare into those two holes . . . even though you have tried to memorize the others' responses, and even though you have told yourself that this time you will pass, when the voice bellows,

Is the

red

dot inside

or

outside

the

white box?

the only thing you can muster is a mumbling of questions, which always go unanswered.

"What red dot?"

"Which white box?

"Have you started yet?"

Con-Fuse-Ion

Each year, as our class filed out of the library, the school nurse would pick up the phone and dial the same phone number that was written on the inside of my lunch box, raincoat, and baseball glove. Then she would tell my mom that I had failed. The call was never a surprise. More of an annual tradition.

But at six years old, I didn't understand what was happening. I had no idea why I couldn't do something that appeared laughably easy for my classmates.

My eyes were a question that went unanswered.

How I See

So why was reading so difficult? And why did the red dot keep disappearing? And what was going on in my brain at such an early age that caused my vision to spiral in this way?

It turns out it's not a problem with my eyes, individually. Both of them work quite well. I have 20/20 vision in each. It's just when it comes to the collaboration part that they have some difficulty.

Most brains receive two images—one from each eye—and then they combine these images into one view. This process is called fusion.

But when I was a baby, and my brain received the two images, it couldn't figure out how to stitch them together. Instead of seeing one combined image, I was seeing two of everything. Two bottles, two pillows, two of every toy. I had to figure out which one was real.

My brain found a solution. It started to ignore information from one eye so it would only have to deal with one of these images at a time.

But the trick had consequences—to this day, in my central vision, I only see out of one eye at a time, and my brain alternates between them every couple of seconds.

So here's why I kept failing that test. The machine showed the red dot to only the left eye and the white box to only the right eye.

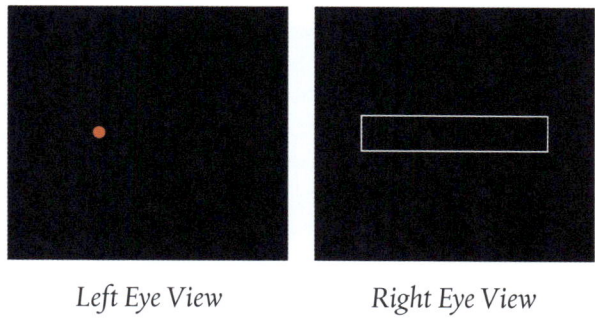

Left Eye View　　　　*Right Eye View*

Everyone else's brains fused these two images together, making the test seem quite obvious.

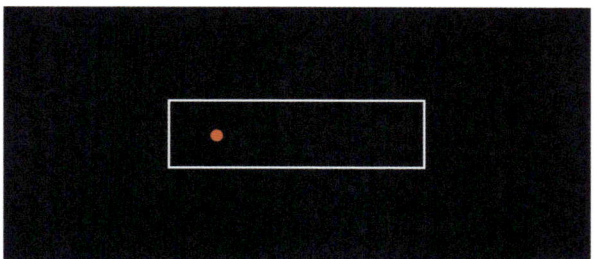

What My Classmates Saw

But my brain could only see the white box. Or the red dot. Never both.

Fuse Your Eyes with Me

You can try this test for yourself, and see if your brain can fuse the red dot and the white box. Fold the page as shown, and put your nose on the red X.

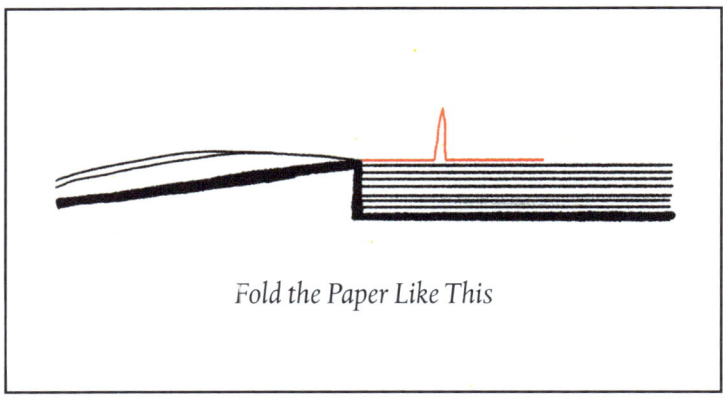

Fold the Paper Like This

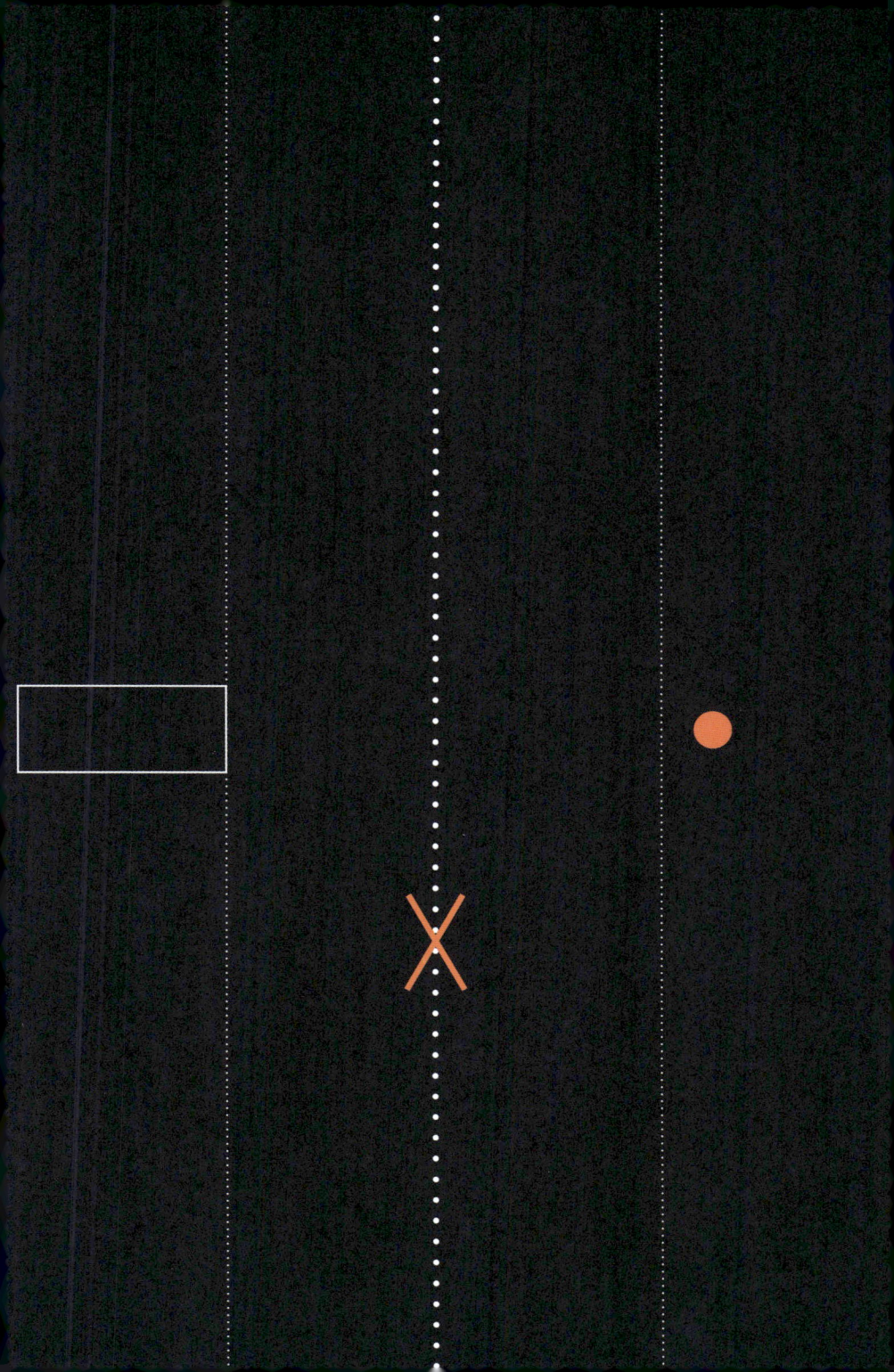

INSTRUCTIONS

1. Bring your face to the book until the tip of your nose is touching the red X on the crease.

2. If you close one eye at a time, you will see my world of alternating vision. Only the red dot. Or the white box.

3. But if you are like most people, when you open both eyes, the red dot will appear to be neatly nested within the white box.

It wasn't until years after my brain had taught itself to look out of one eye at a time that the consequences of my adaptation started to become clear.

Since each eye sees a slightly different view, every time my brain switches between eyes, it looks like my entire world jumps.

The paragraph that
was over here would
suddenly

jump over here
without warning. And
I would need a second
to find

my spot, and
continue reading, only
for all the text on the
page to

jump back over
here. I had no idea the
jumping wasn't normal.

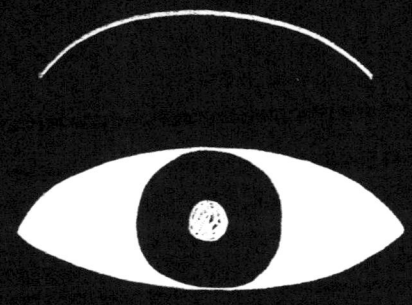

stop.

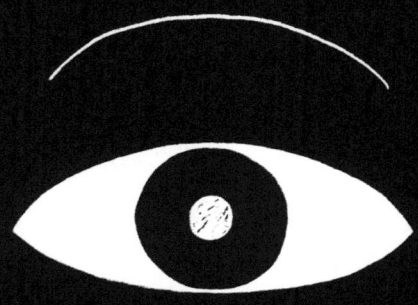

Someone's staring.

👁 👁 They're still staring. It's not a blank stare. But it's not a particularly "present" stare either. It's like when I came home from school, and I had a crusty stain on my white collared shirt. And Mom 👁 👁 wasn't quite sure if it was dried-up ketchup from a hot dog at lunch. Or paint from art class. 👁 👁 Or some other foreign substance that might cause revulsion. And so she stared at it. "What is that?" And she started 👁 👁 to claw at it with cautious disgust . . . 👁 👁 Looking for something that was identifiable. She couldn't hide the look on her face that she was bracing to be repulsed.

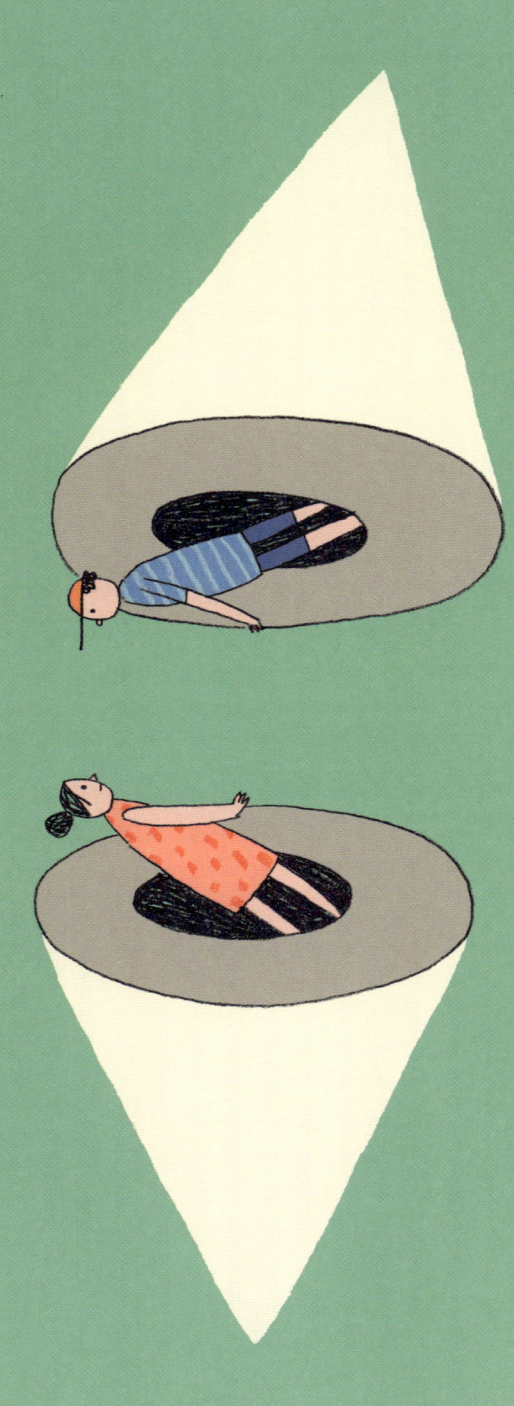

Dear Starer,

Why are you staring? Is it at me?
Is there something caught in
my teeth?

Sincerely,

Eye on the Ball

When my family moved to Tulsa, Oklahoma, we discovered that sports were king. First graders weren't allowed to play tackle football. But my older brother, Kirk, was invited to watch a second-grade tackle football game and witnessed a player break his arm during one of the plays.

"Did he cry?"

"No—that's the thing, he didn't even cry."

"He broke his arm and didn't cry?" I ran to the kitchen. "Mom, did you know that when Harry broke his arm—"

"—he didn't even cry," Mom finished. "Yes, Kirk told me."

Southern sports culture was still foreign to us. But as spring approached, a new season was on the horizon, and we were eager to take part.

I had my eye on baseball. Twice per week, on the way to the science room, our class would walk through the hallway of trophies, which weren't so much proudly displayed as they were tightly crammed together. The tallest ones were my favorite. Topped with a figurine of a baseball player, they rivaled me in height.

What I didn't know at the time was that many of my classmates had been preparing for their baseball careers since long before encountering the mega-trophies. It wasn't uncommon for dads to pitch Ping-Pong balls to their five-year-olds, who batted with broomsticks to hone their aim.

Even though the competition in first grade was a bit more mellow than in the older years, the coaches, parents, and players cared. A lot. And I didn't want to let them down.

There was Taylor, who at three feet, six inches could outrun the entire team. And then, there was Bryce, the coach's son. Even as a six-year-old, when adults spoke about him going pro, they meant it. And they were right. He would go on to play for Stanford, and was later drafted by the San Diego Padres. His first-grade hits were dingers that flew over the heads of shortstops, outfielders, and sometimes, the fence.

Mine weren't.

My first infraction against the team came early in the season. My family didn't bring a snack when it was our turn. Horrified that this might be our doing, I pretended that I, too, was mad at the family who had somehow forgotten, even though what I really felt was a nauseating who-else-could-possibly-have-done-this guilt. When heads hung low during the walk back to the parking lot, what was mourned wasn't the dropped pop fly, or the grounder that snuck between Scott's legs, but instead, the forgotten Gushers.

Catoosa

We didn't realize just how serious all of this really was until months later, when it was time for the playoffs, and my brother's team faced their rival from Catoosa.

Playoffs were a family affair, filled with picnics, pageantry, and popcorn.

Each player's name was announced over the loudspeaker. Parents clapped and whistled as their kids sprang from the chain-linked dugout and proudly lined up next to their teammates on the first-base line. The national anthem blared as—hand over heart—we all sang to an enormous American flag.

Most of the families had shown up with coolers and picnic blankets. Grandparents and cousins. Brownies and Gushers. Unequipped with folding chairs, we sat alone on the bleachers. We were the outsiders: The northerners. The academics. The Democrats.

Although the entire scene was dripping with absurdity, for six- and seven-year-olds, this was the dream. And it felt as if we were important enough to justify all of the fanfare and tradition of the big leagues.

Crowding the opposing baseline, an equally enthusiastic sea of Catoosa fans donned green and black. A few parents had pinned up a giant sign to the chain-link fence: "Catoosa," it read in flowing script that resembled the classic Coca-Cola logo.

As a crackling voice from the loudspeaker announced that it was time to play ball, the first batter from Kirk's team stepped up to the plate. The opposing team's pitcher threw his first pitch—high and outside.

"Ball one," the umpire proclaimed.

That's when things got funky.

Catoosa's head coach walked up to the umpire, showed him a sheet of paper. And then, after a few minutes and a brief conversation with the Monte Cassino coach, the umpire turned to the fans and declared, "That's the game."

Murmurs erupted among parents.

"Disqualified?" The word leapt over coolers and scurried across picnic blankets.

It wasn't until the message was whispered down the line of the concession stand that the answer reached us. The coach from the opposing team had studied the rulebook and found an obscure statement. Students were not allowed to play on the school league and the travel league at the same time. Because this was the playoffs, we were in the one-week period during which the end of the spring school league and the beginning of the summer travel league overlapped.

The opposing coach had not only found the rule but sought out the registration list for the entire summer league, and cross-referenced it with the lineup from my brother's team. Three Monte Cassino players were— unbeknownst to them—breaking the rules by playing for both teams simultaneously.

And rather than saying, "Hey, it's against the rules for three of your players to play in this game," the coach had waited until the first pitch was thrown, so that the entire team would be disqualified. End of game. End of season.

There was an uproar from a few parents.

"You should at least let them play the game," one

grandmother shouted into the empty field.

But Catoosa was already packing up. They weren't there to play. They were there to win.

Eye on the Ball

When it came to sports, I wasn't really used to winning. I had a problem. Here's what would happen when Coach threw me a ball:

When I stood in ready position—with my bat over my shoulder and feet lined up with the plate—I would stare at the ball out of the corner of my left eye.

But when it was time to swing, I shifted my shoulders so they faced the pitcher, and now my left eye was looking far off into left field—not at the ball. So, midway through my swing, my right eye would take over. Because my eyes pointed in slightly different directions, each time my eyes switched, the world jumped.

The baseball that was

here

is suddenly

here . . . ?

or

maybe

somewhere

in

between?

It felt hopeless. But it was also first grade—forgiveness was embedded within the rules. We played a hybrid of T-ball and baseball. First, the coach would pitch you two balls, and you would try your best to thwack them. If you couldn't thwack 'em, then you would have two tries on the tee. The tee is something like an oversized golf tee: It holds the ball still, right in front of you, right at thwacking height.

The plan was as generous as it was simple—everyone was guaranteed a hit.

Game Time

It's the middle of the season, and we're playing against Marquette. Once again, I am batting second to last.

As I step up to the plate, I see Coach kneeling a few feet in front of the mound, holding the ball up, right at eye level, making sure I can see it. He tosses a soft lob at chest height. It is slow and has a nice arc to it. I step and swing. Nothing but air.

"A bit early on that one," someone shouts.

Coach holds up another ball and lobs it. Again, I step and swing. I hear the ball hit the catcher's mitt before my swing is complete. "A bit high, James."

Coach jogs off the field and grabs the tee, placing it right over the plate, the ball balancing neatly on top.

I step up to the tee and let loose with a big whoosh. I look out into the field, trying to find where my ball went, only to glance back down at the tee. There it is, gleaming like an Easter egg.

"Striiiiiiike," the umpire bellows.

"Oooh, close," the parents echo.

"Eye on the ball," Dad shouts from the bleachers.

I have one last chance. I hold the bat up. I take my step forward. I twist my back foot and squash the bug just like they taught me. I rotate my shoulders. My eyes switch as I take my swing. I look out onto the field.

Nothing.

Not a cheer. Not a "Good job." Not a whistle.

And the ball is there. Again. Sitting on the stick.

The umpire isn't sure what to do.

The coaches whisper to each other, confused by the rules.

"Good try—you'll get it next time," chirps Coach, signaling it is time to head back to the dugout.

The coach's older son is in third grade, and helps to keep us organized on the bench. But he had been deep in debate about the merits of Cheetos versus Cheez-Its and had missed the whole ordeal. He turned to let me know I was on deck.

I told him I already went. "What happened?"

"Oh, I struck out," I said nonchalantly.

"Struck out? But you can't strike out. They're supposed to let you hit it off—" He hopped up to get his dad's attention, ready to interrupt the game, but was promptly told to sit down.

Strikingly Different

The T-ball strikeout and my subsequent performance that season were a wake-up call: I was not what I seemed.

I was going to face the public humiliation that comes with being different. And one thing seemed certain. I couldn't just pack my bags after one pitch and declare victory on a technicality. I was going to have to work through this difference in front of a crowd that was cheering and chanting my name, while having no idea why I couldn't just hit the darn ball.

James

Today is Monday March 10
2003.

A life skill that I am
using is hope.

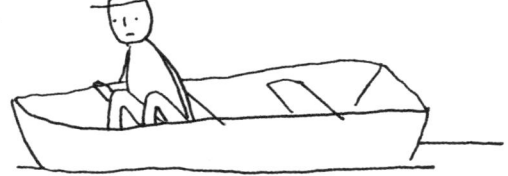

Drifting

As I progressed through school, my eyes began to change. Each year, as I got a few inches taller, my eyes drifted a few degrees farther apart. Unlike in my infancy, when they were crossed, this time, they were slowly drifting outward. The spread was inevitable.

I had two surgeries in my infancy. The hope was that after aligning my eyes surgically, they would learn to move as a team as my brain discovered how to fuse their images together. That didn't happen. But the surgery did give me the look of normalcy, at least for a few years.

As my condition became more noticeable, I became more noticed. First grade had brought my first stares.

In second grade, my eyes were pointed just slightly outward. But it felt like the world was going out of its way to reaffirm my normalcy.

In the middle of that year, my family moved again, this time to the suburbs of Chicago.

On one of my first days of school, students were called to the table at the back of the room for a reading assessment. One by one, each received a nod of approval and sat back down.

And then it was my turn. I stumbled through the paragraph. Then tried again. Partway through my third reading, I was saved by the bell.

But not really, because the next day, the teacher called me back for a fourth and fifth reading. By round six, I had memorized the trouble spots, allowing me to finish the passage under the time limit.

In my new teacher's eyes, she had done me a favor: I passed; she had spared me the shame of special education.

By third grade, my misaligned eyes were noticeable if you really stared. But for the most part, it wasn't a big deal.

I spent weekends throwing the baseball back and forth with my dad, and evenings reading out loud to my mom. Dad worked the crossover, challenging me to reach across my body for the satisfactory and solid thwack of ball-in-glove.

Mom worked the Magic Tree House, cutting little windows in index cards so that the words wouldn't jump away. As Annie and Jack spun, I tested eye patches, glasses, and bookmarks that I would slide down the page to help the words stay still.

When my eyes came up in family conversation, my parents would remind me, "You have special eyes," with excitement and mystery—always hinting that there were things that I could do that they couldn't.

As fourth grade turned to fifth, and fifth to sixth, my eyes drifted straight into public domain. Classmates, friends, and teachers noticed.

"James, are you with us?" teachers needled.

"What is up with your eye?" classmates would ask.

"Is it glass?" I was asked several times on the bus, dashing hopes that I would remove my eye from its socket on demand.

My older brother began getting questions from classmates and mutual friends who were too shy to ask me. Each time the topic was broached, a group of bobbling and curious heads would gather round.

My secret was becoming a spectacle.

The thing is, when you start to explain your eyes, you become a sort of museum specimen. Like a piece of modern art that someone looks at with confusion and disapproval and says, "Is this really art?"

It comes with an eye contact that stops abruptly at the surface of your face. They're looking at you. But not into you. And I could feel them wavering, back and forth. Compelled and repulsed.

How is it possible

and yet

so unseen?

I was learning that I needed a script. What my friends wanted was an answer—something short and repeatable.

But I didn't have answers. I could barely remember what the eye doctor had called it during annual checkups. "It's something like ex—, exo . . . something. It begins with an *X*," I would say.

I was searching for *exotropia*.

During one such episode, my bumbling was interrupted.

"—No ya don't," Ryan declared. "You have a lazy eye."

I was surprised, not so much by the interjection as by the reaction. Instead of puzzled looks, or confusion, classmates had an immediate level of acceptance.

A lazy eye was something that they had heard of. And though it did nothing to explain my condition or how to look at me, it seemed to satiate their desire: a quick I've-heard-of-this explanation.

"Oh, you have a lazy eye?" someone responded.

I hesitated and gave in. "Yeah, it's a lazy eye."

Ryan gifted me with a way out. A crowd-proof deflector that passed the familiarity test. It was, of course, not true. But my grade-school job wasn't to explain my eyes; it was to satisfy the needs of the crowd.

Within the span of a few years, my invisible secret had turned into the first thing most people noticed about me. Even if someone didn't know my name or age or whose class I was in, they knew I was the kid with the eyes.

Dear Starer,

Have you found what you're looking for?

Sincerely,

Hurry Up and Wait

The life of a suburban middle schooler has two speeds—*hurry up* and *wait*.

When it's time to *hurry up*, it feels like everything is your fault. The world is waiting on you. There's an excitement in the air, but it's an excitement that can easily spin toward panic.

Each morning, as my 6:50 alarm beeped at full throttle, I awoke with a tingling sense of pride. Not only had I remembered to turn on my alarm the night before, but other than Dad, who had to be out the door by 5:30, I was the first one up: a feat that demanded announcement. Tromping down the stairs with sufficient clatter to make my presence heard, I would slip in an extra squeak as I rounded the loose floorboard outside of Kirk's room. I had at least ten minutes on him, and I knew it.

At 6:55, I set the shower alarm for four and a half minutes. The alarm was a "gift" to my brother, whose habit of vertical sleep under a pulsing stream of steaming water tended to exhaust the hot water supply. The shower is not the time for *wait*.

At 7:05, I shifted my focus to my newfound responsibility. While my mother made lunches and attempted to extract my older brother from bed, I was put in charge of prepping my four-year-old brother for school.

My parents had found that for the same price as American play-dough-and-finger-paint preschool, they could enroll my brother in the local French immersion school.

Each morning, he was required to don a pristine uniform: blue pants, a white collared shirt, and their trademark sweater, *le pull rouge*. I had been told that Reed's French school experience would benefit all of us. In fact, I had chosen to take French in school, with the promise that if I ever tripped up over grammar, I could turn to our resident four-year-old for help.

But French school made Reed a French *puriste*, and

rather than help, he snarled at my American accent. I seemed to be the only one who thought he was becoming a bit too French.

By the time my older brother and I had devoured our breakfast, brushed our teeth, forgotten to take our vitamins, been recalled to the kitchen by our hawk-eyed mother, only to limp toward the door with shoelaces flailing, any pride from the early morning wake-up-to-your-own-alarm accomplishment had long faded.

We left the house together, slamming the crooked door behind us—not because we were angry but because that was the only way to close it. As Mom buckled the family French fry into his car seat, Kirk and I crossed the street and tried to leave all that morning business behind us. Not that you really could.

Everyone at the bus stop overheard each other's morning drama. It created a sense of camaraderie among fellow bus-stoppees—a sympathy fostered through shared defeats. They witnessed our mom frantically running down the driveway, waving two forgotten lunch boxes overhead. We heard their parents say "I love you" and force them to say it back with a kiss.

There was unity in our early morning disorganization.

And perhaps the only thing that really separated the Robinson-family chaos from the Logan-family chaos was that when we shouted, "Hurry up" to our four-year-old, it was in French.

Wait

At the bus stop, you got to switch modes. It was now time to *wait*.

There wasn't much to do in *wait*. But it meant you were secure. Safe. Unbothered. You had passed. And now it was time to pass time. When you were in *hurry up*, heads turned. But when you were in *wait*, they stared off into space.

Waiting meant winning. Waiting meant you were ahead. Or perhaps more importantly—it meant that someone else was behind.

At twelve, we began to develop a primal need to see someone else ranked below us. *Wait* was the safest place to be. Because as long as *you* were in *wait*, it meant that *someone else* was in *hurry up*.

Hurry up was often under the watchful eye of a teacher or adult. But waiting was something we were beginning to do on our own. There were boundaries and rules. No shouting. Stay in line. When you wait at the bus stop, don't talk to strangers.

Most mornings, we stood in secure proximity to our block's stop sign. Usually in silence. Accompanied by a few neighbors. Waiting for the school bus on brisk, suburban-Illinois mornings.

The bus would weave its way through the same grid that extends through all midwestern towns. Two streets down, it would pass from left to right. That meant we had seven minutes. One street down, it would pass from right to left. Two minutes to go.

School

The rhythm of the school day echoed the morning: Hurry up, wait . . . wait, hurry up. We had the same schedule every day. Forty-five-minute classes separated by five minutes spent waiting in the hall for the next one to begin. We had to walk in lines everywhere. Even at twelve, you were uncooperative if you stepped out of line.

When we were in elementary school, we cared about the class. The class got a pizza party for good behavior.

The class performed together. Or sang together. Or blew on the recorder, making the sound of a hundred dying elephants—together.

But in middle school, we started to see ourselves as individuals. Competition wasn't just between classes but also within them. Every lesson, test, quiz, and activity had a winner. It wasn't the person who scored the highest—we wouldn't find that out until days later. It wasn't the person who showed the most improvement or growth.

Instead, the person who gained the most social points was the one who finished first. During a test, they would stand up, look around the room—down at all the faces still buried in their papers—and then walk their test to the teacher. Back at their seat, they would read their book. Or doodle. Or dig into their desk, allowing the squeaking of the lid to announce to the rest of the class that they were done: waiting for each and every one of us to hurry up.

With this new form of competition came a new form of shame. There were few worse social positions you could find yourself in than being stuck in *hurry up* while everyone else was in *wait*.

Takashi

In middle school, one of my closest friends was Takashi. Much like myself, Takashi was relatively new. His father's job was transferred from Tokyo to Chicago, meaning he was facing a lot of news—new friends, new school, new teachers, new language. It was that last one that tripped up my classmates. Their impatience was palpable when he needed to search for words. So he kept his sentences short. I watched in frozen sympathy as they underestimated him, conflating his English ability with intelligence.

There was a camaraderie between us. We both knew what it meant to be on the wrong side of *hurry up*. In many ways, Takashi endured the worst of what I was trying to avoid.

One morning, we each had to report how many math flash cards we had completed in two minutes. Our parents were supposed to test us. "How many cards, Takashi?" the teacher asked.

"Ninety," he said.

"In two minutes?" the teacher asked.

"Yep," he chirped with a quick head nod. That was nearly fifteen cards more than anyone else in the class.

"More like thirty minutes," Kayleigh whispered to a neighbor. A round of smirks confirmed the table's agreement.

My lingering regret is that I never actually stood up for Takashi. Maybe I felt like I couldn't. Although I did stand by him, which felt equally important at the time.

I was indebted to him for more than friendship. When it came to reading, Takashi was the slowest. And I was the second slowest. He gave me a buffer. And a license to take my time.

* * * *

Midway through sixth grade, Takashi's family moved back to Japan.

At his going-away party—a collection of cookies and doughnuts—Sarah proclaimed, "H-e-y, T-a-k-a-s-h-i-, w-e h-a-v-e d-o-u-g-h-n-u-t-s b-y t-h-e w-h-i-t-e-b-o-a-r-d." She spoke the words so slowly that it sounded as if she was talking to a dog rather than a classmate.

Takashi and I ate our doughnuts side by side. Backs up against the cabinet, looking over a class that was relieved there would no longer be so much waiting.

Tomorrow, without Takashi, I would face their impatience alone.

Testing

A few months after Takashi left, the ISATS, the annual state achievement test, loomed.

In preparation, I was given two accommodations. First, I would receive time and a half. And second, I was allowed to circle my answers in the test booklet and someone else would transfer the responses to the bubble sheet. For those with tracking issues, the bubble sheet is a hellhole. On practice tests, I had lost much-needed time scrambling to erase and re-bubble after discovering I had missed a row. Only to realize the booklet and bubble sheet numbers still weren't lining up.

The accommodations were a huge help.

But, there was a catch. Even though I was given extra time, I would still have to take the bulk of the test in the regular classroom with the rest of my classmates.

Each section of the ISATS was sixty-five minutes long. But if the whole class was done within fifty-five minutes, you were allowed to start your break early. The thing was,

I wouldn't be allowed to go to the extra-time room unless I had sat for the full sixty-five minutes.

When all this was explained to me, it seemed pretty straightforward. I would just use all my time and then keep going. But in practice, it feels different. Have a seat at my desk.

40 minutes into the reading test, Drew closes his test booklet and takes out his library book.

44 minutes. You look up briefly. Two more classmates have finished.

47 minutes. Nearly half the class has closed their test booklet. You're in the second half.

50 minutes. There are three of you.

53 minutes. Now you're the only one left. You can feel the needles on your face. Each time you look up, a new face is staring at you. First Kayleigh. Then John. But if you wait out these next ten minutes, you'll be able to focus in the room without the stares.

55 minutes have passed. Two students in the front row stand up to stretch and start to groan. "Shhhhhhh," the teacher shushes.

"Who is still work—"

"Quiet," Ms. Gordon demands. Teachers also hated the race to finish first since their performance would be judged by the scores.

57 minutes. You can't pretend to ignore the faces. They're no longer reading their books. Just staring up at the clock. And back at you. Up at the clock. And back at you.

60 minutes. Five to go.

Charlie—normally a friend—is sitting directly in front of you. You spent much of the test staring at the back of his chair. He turns around and stares, right at your test.

You look up. *Hurry up*, he mouths.

You can no longer read. Or think. Up at the clock and back at you.

You've answered only one question in the final passage.

61 minutes.

You reread the question. The cacophony of squirming has hijacked your brain. Do you just turn it in unfinished? The sweat suggests that's the easiest way out. But they might take away your accommodation.

64 minutes. Ms. Gordon walks up to your desk, leans by your side, and asks if you want to go to the extra-time room.

As one final stretch of indignity, you get up and stand by the door, test in hand. Ms. Gordon gets on the phone to the extra-time room, to tell them that she is sending one their way. And alas, you are free from the stares, free from the *hurry up*. Or so you think.

Just before Ms. Gordon closes the door, you hear the exhale of a class that has finally been released.

And one word, puffed out by a classmate, or maybe several . . . "*Finally . . .*"

Sometimes the stares   feel like

a thousand little pokes.   Like

acupuncture coming from all directions.

Spikes that you

want to stop

by closing your eyes.

Wherever you go,

the eyes are there.

Twisted necks

giving double glances.

They are
questioning

Confused.

Uncertain.

You can hear the voice within their head, asking, *What is wrong with you?*

And as you sit awkwardly in the discomfort of their stare, you resist the urge to ask them the same.

I Don't Care

In Suburbiaville, there is a cultural ritual that parents perform when trying to get a group picture of children. The first photograph is the serious picture. Same with the second. It will be sent to Nan and Uncle Bill. The kids need to look nice: Pleasant smiles are all that are permissible.

"Say cheese," parents call out from behind the camera.

A choir of cheeses echoes.

Cheeky grins.

Dimples on full display.

Sometimes, the voice from behind the camera tries to surprise.

"Say cucumber!"

"Enchilada!"

"Tequila!" Anything to get a half laugh. There were

always a few voices that would still say cheese no matter the requested verbiage.

But the good behavior displayed in the first two pictures was always riding on the promise of the third: the goofy picture.

The third picture is when you stick out your tongue, give your neighbor bunny ears, or make an ugly face. For many, the third picture is when you cross your eyes.

You might think that this was something that brought me terrible anguish as a child. That on the third photograph, as I looked around at my friends contorting their faces to make them look like my own, I would feel hurt and isolated and objectified.

But when it was time to take the silly photo, I joined the competition. I laughed as I tried to push my eyes further into orientations that connoted "crazy," "wild," "silly," and all the other things that our parents didn't want us to be. With my hands enthusiastically squishing my face and my eyes strained, I became an active participant in the degradation of my own self-image.

Uncaring

Looking back, I'm not surprised. I didn't want to think about my eyes. I wanted to be normal. Take normal pictures. Do as normal does.

In fact, nearly every eye-related event that I have mentioned so far—the strikeout, the red dot, the upside-down book, the long walk to the extra-time room—wasn't mentioned in the car on the way home. Or at the kitchen table. Instead, these moments were suppressed on the spot.

I had found the ready-made solution to my eye issue. When people stared, I would reassure myself that I just didn't care.

If I didn't care about my eyes, I couldn't be offended when someone looked over their shoulder and then asked, "Are you talking to me?" I couldn't be bothered by any name-calling or off-kilter remarks. If I didn't care about my eyes, then I wouldn't feel the burden of trying to get other people to care about them too.

Indifference was a source of protection. You can't hurt someone by attacking something they do not care about.

It also was the easiest out. It requires no action or

intervention. I didn't have to hold anyone accountable or disrupt anyone's preconceptions.

But what I did not fully grasp was that by deciding on indifference—by making the choice to not care—I was also choosing to surrender. I was giving away any power that I had over the moment in which my eyes were perceived. And I was pushing it into the hands of those who were staring. Those who didn't know how to look me in the eye.

The truth about not caring is that it can be dangerous. It breeds anger. And frustration. And it can take you to places that you don't even realize you're going.

Dear Starer,

Do you know how repetitive it is to get stared at?

It's the same thing every day.

But really, I don't care.

Until next time,

Fixation

When I reached middle school, my inner turmoil was up for public debate. No longer an unnoticed underperformer, I was suddenly pegged as a high-priority fixer-upper. I was advised to wait until high school to have my third surgery. In the meantime, teachers, friends, and friends of friends provided advice, backed up by the one thing that they could offer—anecdotes.

There was always a brother or a cousin who had faced similar challenges and was successfully fixed with this treatment, or that special program, or some homegrown bag of tricks.

As my reading level continued to lag in school, the anecdotes got messier. Everyone wanted to fix me. They began putting forward strategies that weren't always backed by science. The desire to fix overpowered the desire to help.

Anecdotes can be powerful. They feed hope and give the provider a sense of providing. But anecdotes are the story of a single person. Critical details are often glossed over or left out completely. Outcomes are rarely as replicable as the story may lead you to believe.

And yet I believed in them. Each one, as it came my way. Because they were the only things I could believe in.

Model Student

Ms. Betts told my parents the story of one of her students, who had gone to a therapist to relearn his ABCs by modeling each letter in clay. He was dyslexic, and it had turned him from a reluctant reader into a voracious one. I wasn't dyslexic, but the therapist thought that it could still help my reading. So I, too, began warming sticks of modeling clay in my hands and rolling them into worms. Worms became letters as I worked to arrange the floppy characters into my "trouble" words. I modeled *the* and *there* and read them forward and backward in an attempt to rewire my brain. The clay smelled. It reeked.

The greasy vowels and consonants left smears on my little brother's plastic place mats. After two months of no progress, the oily mess retreated to a cabinet.

,   ,

Then there was the eye doctor, who told me that I could learn to speed-read if I changed my attitude. All I had to do was read between the commas.

Turning the anecdote on herself, she explained how she, too, had struggled to read, although she was never an alternator. With the comma trick, she could now speed-read with ease.

She handed me a book.

"Just read between the commas."

It was open to a random page. I tried jumping between the commas. I grabbed words as fast as I could. I ran my finger down the page until I hit bottom, and looked up.

"See, you're getting the hang of it," she reassured me.

I had no idea what I had read.

Pointers

One English teacher thought he could fix me by getting me to use my index finger while reading.

"You know, even today when I read, I sometimes use my finger," Mr. Anderson told me as he held up his book, dragging his extended pointer finger down the center of the page, as if I had never before heard of the concept.

When he hovered over my shoulder during quiet reading, I would extend my index finger and drag. But when he went back to his desk, I would switch and point with my middle finger.

Some people will try to convince you that only the rude people stare. But that's not true. Everybody stares. It is human to stare. We stare at the things that alarm us. The things that seem out of place. We stare at what we've never seen before. What burns is the fact that you are worthy of being stared at.

Dear Starer,

Can I be honest?
If I didn't have these eyes,
I would probably stare too.

Anyway. I hope you find what
you're looking for.

3D

There was no story more tantalizing than that of Sue Barry. When I was in sixth grade, she published a book called *Fixing My Gaze*. It was the perfect anecdote.

Like me, Sue saw out of one eye at a time, and she described in her book how, after months of eye exercises, she could suddenly use her eyes together to see in 3D.

Sue's book defied years of scientific belief. But to explain why, I need to share a bit about depth perception.

What does it mean to see the world as flat?

you may ask me.

Well, what does it mean to see the world in 3D?

I would ask you.

If I were to place this book on a table, open to this page, and try to touch the tip of my pointer finger to the red asterisk,

my strategy would probably be different from yours. That's because your eyes likely have a power that mine do not: the ability to work together to judge depth.

As I bring my index finger toward the page, I predict the moment of contact by watching the shadow of my finger come closer and closer to the red asterisk. But outside of the shadow, and relative size, I mostly judge depth by guessing.

Most people don't have to guess. Instead, they automatically "know" how far away the page is from their finger by seeing and sensing this depth. This ability to perceive how objects protrude into space is like a superpower. It's called stereoscopic vision.

If you have it, then you use your stereoscopic vision every day. It helps you turn the pages of this book, walk down the sidewalk, and effortlessly shake an outstretched hand. Stereoscopic vision is like a little miracle of human perception. Without it, things can get awkward.

Fusion

The first step in gaining this superpower is fusion. You were already fusing when you looked at the red dot and the white box. Your brain saw two different images and combined them, putting the red dot inside the white box.

Most eye doctors believe that your brain learns to fuse images during the first few years of life, and that after that, if you have never experienced stereoscopic vision, it's too late for your brain to learn how.

But Sue's experiences as an adult appeared to defy this belief. After a vision therapy appointment, as she settled into the seat of her car, the steering wheel suddenly appeared to be floating in front of her. Rather than her usual view of it—flat against the dashboard—she could actually see the space behind it. It was popping out, right there, in front of her.

Shocked, she closed one eye, and all went back to normal: The steering wheel was flat against the dashboard. But when she reopened her eye, there it was, floating in space. At first her bouts of 3D vision lasted only a few minutes. They were startling: A grape in her salad suddenly became indescribably round. A giant skeleton of a horse that she walked past every day on the way to her lab burst into three dimensions, causing her to jump. Sue's world was expanding into a new dimension. And even though she had thought little of stereoscopic vision when she didn't have it, she was finding it to be life-changing.

As a middle schooler, I didn't understand the intricacies of her case—or even my own. I knew that most people could "see in 3D." And I knew that I couldn't. But I connected to her story. I wanted to be a person who, because of his hard work and determination, was able to fix his vision. I wanted to become an anecdote. Sue's story of overcoming gave me something that can be as dangerous as it is motivating: hope.

My X

Dr. Zane's office looked like a carnival frozen in time. Shelves with strange-looking children's toys lined one wall. A row of chairs were tucked under a counter, facing a series of red and green posters. In the center of the room was a large board with three concentric circles of buttons. The array looked like a control panel that you might see at a power plant or on a space shuttle.

I would later learn that this machine was designed to improve your ability to track and locate objects. Each time you pressed a button, another one would light up, and you would have to find and press it as quickly as possible. The large crack down the center of the board suggested that one patient had been so enthusiastic with their slamming of the buttons that they had broken through the machine.

Dr. Zane was tall and clean in his white lab coat.

"Have a seat," he said, pulling out two chairs.

I sat down at the counter as he took the seat next to me.

This was new. At nearly every other intervention—every doctor's office and therapist and special education meeting—I had to sit across from the doctor, or therapist, or teacher: face-to-face. In those meetings, the physical arrangement of our bodies had been intimidating and confrontational.

But Dr. Zane and I were sitting side by side. Teammates and equals. We were in this together. After years of walking out of offices as a failure who was too young for an intervention or too old to be fixed, I had finally found someone who was in my time and on my team. Perhaps what I wanted more than anything was a teammate.

Goals

Although Dr. Zane didn't promise me anything, results felt within reach. He made the tests fun, even though I was to fail nearly every one of them. Some tests were new. Others were all too familiar.

He handed me a pair of tinted glasses and opened the standard vinyl booklet: the fly test. "Can you pinch the wing of the fly?" he asked. For those with stereoscopic vision, a giant fly appears to hover a few inches over the booklet, giving them the sensation that the object is really there, popping out from the page. I'd imagine it would be rather off-putting to suddenly find oneself in the company of a fly that was larger than your hand. Fortunately, I didn't have to worry about that. For those of us without stereoscopic vision, the fly looks no different whether the glasses are on or off.

Pinching is impossible, since the fly remains flat within the page. So I decided I would tap the wing with my index finger and thumb placed together as if I was holding a pencil.

"Good," he said.

They never tell you when you've failed. But you always know it.

Brock String

My visits became weekly, with each session's homework building on the last. It was like training for a sport. Lots of reps. Right eye. Left eye. Up. Down. Side to side.

After one such session, I was sent home with a cord coiled in a plastic baggie: the holy grail of vision therapy—my Brock String.

It's a simple tool, featuring three beads—one green, one yellow, and one red. The contraption is meant to teach you to bring your eyes together—to focus both eyes on one of the beads—and, hopefully, entice your brain to fuse the images from each eye.

If you have stereoscopic vision, when you hold one end of the string to your nose and focus your eyes on the bead in the middle, the string will appear as an X.

You can try this for yourself by holding the book flat on the table and then raising it to eye level. Keep your eyes just a few inches from the page and focus on the yellow dot.

Hold the book out flat at eye level,

a few inches from your face, and stare at the yellow dot.

My goal for the next few months would be to see that X. I spent twenty minutes a day holding the string to my nose—Mom on the other end, holding it to hers. We pulled the string taut. We compared views. When my mom stared at the center bead, she could see an X. I couldn't. I could just see one string.

Tightrope

Ten months into vision therapy, I was making scattered bits of progress. My eye muscles were growing stronger. I could now bring my eyes together to look "normal" momentarily. When doing so, my vision would blur, so I couldn't see much—and it hurt—but I could finally make my eyes look straight—at least for a photograph.

And that mattered. If not to me, then to those looking at the picture.

One incredibly hot afternoon while drooped on the porch, Brock String held to my nose—Mom's nose glued to the other end—I sensed a slight quivering. Pulling taut, I stared at the bead. My eyes were switching back and forth quickly; the string was jumping from the left to the right. Then, for a few flashy seconds, I saw a flicker of a V.

Both arms at the same time.

I croaked out in an empty, dry voice, "Wait, I think it might be working."

My mom cracked a smile on the other end. "Okay, keep holding it," she said. "Don't move."

After months of daily string staring, neither of us wanted to curse the moment.

"Whoaaa," I whispered.

"Is it still there?"

"A little bit . . ." I looked up at her, lowering the string from my face and blinking repeatedly. It was as if I was a toddler, having just taken my first steps. I stared back at the bead that was closest, the strings flickered back and forth, and then they held. Two strings at once. My eyes must be working together.

It felt like the hard work was beginning to pay off. I would finally be able to show up to Dr. Zane's office with some good news.

The sensation lasted only a few seconds at first. But those seconds carried me for weeks.

Even the emotionless Dr. Zane cracked a smile and seemed energized. With a jaunty pace, he disappeared down the hallway, returning with a catalogue. He excitedly flipped through the pages, and with a red Sharpie, circled the new piece of equipment he would order.

VEXED

I was seeing the V while staring at the bead that was closest to me. The next step was to stare at the middle bead. Here, I was supposed to see an X.

But each time I shifted my gaze from the closest bead to the middle one, the two strings would turn back into one.

I tried staring at the string for even longer. But the X wouldn't pop into focus. I just couldn't see it.

After months of struggling for the elusive X, my mom wanted answers. "So what can we do?" she asked Dr. Zane.

He paused. Started to talk and then paused some more. Dr. Zane was gentle and quiet. You never knew what he was going to say. And he always withheld judgment and withheld emotion.

"Well, you can try surgery." It was a surprising admission. In our experience, the surgeons and the vision therapists were in different camps, rarely recommending each other. To have a vision therapist recommend surgery after months of what felt like gradual progress was a gut punch.

Even though I had seen the V, even though I had put in the hard work, I had still failed. We had come full circle.

NEXT

Sue Barry's story taught me about an unspoken side of anecdotes. That they can be as devastating as they are motivating. This isn't to blame Sue—after all, *I* was the one who dreamed of making her experience my own. But it's not surprising that Sue's story was the one that arrived in a package at our front door. Stories that fix are the ones that sell.

The hidden counter-story, however, is real. In the process of ingesting her words, I absorbed a broader narrative. It wasn't enough to learn to live with my eyes. I had to change them, fix them, transform how I see. It led me to believe that my story was only worthwhile if, when I stared at the middle bead, the string split into two strands.

I will note that many doctors believe that Sue Barry likely had a stereoscopic event in her early childhood and rather than gaining stereopsis for the first time as an adult, she was *regaining* this ability. Whatever the case, while vision therapy does appear to be helpful for some people, Dr. Zane declared it time for me to give up.

Eventually, I would visit three eye surgeons. I learned that I had a rare complication that put me at an elevated risk for permanent double vision after surgery. Yet for many patients, including adults, eye surgery is a great option. I've included some more information about surgery in the back of this book—noting how my own story would have been different with today's technology.

But back then, after so many failures, and the conflicting opinions of three surgeons, we decided to hold off on surgery, at least for the time being.

It felt like I had exhausted every outlet. And I had nothing but exhaustion to show for it. So I made a decision: I would learn to live with my eyes, instead of trying to fix them.

Mom

By the time I was in middle school, many of my peers had caught the reading bug. There was Liam, who devoured Harry Potter at six years old. And Miles, who always had a book in his back pocket. The love of reading was like a virus that spread throughout the neighborhood, infecting kids near and far. But no matter how many times I tried to get exposed and infected, it appeared that I was immune.

Realness

Yatcheddd.

Eeyyyy-ackt.

Yate.

Yaked.

Yashed.

Yuh-cht.

Yack'td.

Yaught.

I will never own a yacht.

There is a particular sting that comes with the realization that the stories you are being asked to read are meant for third and fourth graders when you are in fifth.

My problem with school wasn't merely my difficulty with the mechanics of reading. It wasn't just the fatigue or the spacing out or the poor comprehension.

My problem was also that I had lost the desire to read. At school, everything seemed to be pretend. It was as if we were playing house and what we did had no impact on or connection to the real world.

We were stuck in this pattern of "hurry up and

learn—but wait until you're a grown-up to sink your teeth into reality."

Because it wasn't real, the motivation for learning was prodded with light threats.

"Your teachers in seventh grade aren't going to be kind like I am."

"Just wait till you get to high school."

I couldn't see where it would end.

Professor Mom

As boring as school can be at twelve years old, it's a rather exciting age to be a human. There are little sparks going off in your head. You start to care about things. For the first time, you can begin to feel the direction you want to follow in life. And that direction is more than just a first-grade, major-league pipe dream. You can begin to follow through on the things that make you curious. Things that make you ask questions. Things that make you think, *This might be who I am.*

My mom became an expert at turning these little sparks of inspiration into flames.

Perhaps she had always been an expert. While

training to become an architect, she fell in love with teaching. She had a knack for distilling complex math and abstract theories into tangible, relatable lectures.

While teaching architecture at the Rhode Island School of Design, she gave her students space to meander through unrefined thoughts and half-baked ideas, helping them identify the tiny granule of clarity that could form the basis of a powerful project. Through pointed questions and subtle clues, she helped her students find their thesis. In the classroom. And in life.

When Mom gave birth to Kirk and me, things began to change. Kirk, two years ahead of me, also had difficulty with reading. He was dyslexic. And although he struggled at school, at home his ingenuity was clear. He could draw anything in three dimensions. And he built all sorts of contraptions with spare parts. The family favorite was a bicycle helmet that delivered potato chips to his mouth at the pull of a cord.

When he was in first grade, Kirk was given an aptitude test at a local elementary school—a place he had never been before. The test administrator asked him, "Where does the sun set?"

Kirk got out of his chair and walked to the window.

He found the sun, and then looked to the horizon, checking back and forth. Finally, he decided, "Over there," and pointed westward.

The test administrator explained to my mom that although he had, indeed, pointed to the west, she had marked his answer as incorrect. The correct answer was a word. *West.* There were no points for pointing.

It became clear that Kirk's genius wasn't being seen at school. And rather than intervene, the school seemed to be taking a back seat.

At a beginning-of-the-year parent-teacher conference, when my mom pushed to discuss the intricacies of Kirk's difficulties with reading, she was met with the resistance of a teacher who preferred to speak in loftier terms.

"It's as if you have boarded an airplane to Paris," Ms. Pickering explained. "And as the plane is descending, you look out the window and see tulips and windmills. And you think, *Wait, this doesn't look like Paris.* Instead, you've landed in Holland."

She continued to point out all of the wonderful things that can happen when you accept a vacation in Amsterdam, instead of Paris.

Ms. Pickering passed the anecdote off as her own concoction—a spur-of-the-moment metaphor. But she was referencing a poem that is often shared among the parents of children with disabilities. Perhaps she thought it was enough that in her version, she had swapped out Rome for Paris. The sentiment of the metaphor isn't entirely insulting. It's true that part of the disability experience involves coming to terms with abilities that are physically or neurologically challenging. Milestones need to be relevant and appropriate. I will always have trouble with baseball.

But to my mom, that went without saying. What she sensed was something else: that the metaphor was being used as an excuse. She felt they were unnecessarily lowering the bar not so much for Kirk—but for themselves. It was easier—and cheaper—to treat the parents' emotions than the child's condition.

It's also worth noting that if you ever do find yourself aboard a plane to Paris that instead lands in Holland, EU regulations stipulate that the airline is required to cover the cost of transit to your ticketed destination.

Still, Mom faced a problem. Between the aptitude test and the trip to Holland, it was becoming clear that no level of advocacy would change the school. If Kirk and I were going to learn, she would have to take the matter into her own hands, continuing to spearhead our education by herself. So she made a decision that would change Kirk's life—and also mine. She put her career on pause, and began teaching us intensively.

Mom set up a long, low desk on the stair landing outside our room. Kirk and I were each perched on a stool, and she sat on the floor between us. The three of us were side by side, at eye level. Teammates.

It was here where Mom invented tools. She helped us practice our math facts with "finger stones" and phonics with hand-illustrated cards.

Sitting on her lap aboard the green, pilled chair that was passed down from my great-grandmother, we switched off—reading every other word—as we found our way through our first books. It was Mom who had us working phonics and sounding out the letters. And it was Mom, not the school, who taught the two of us to read.

She created contraptions and contests. She lured Kirk and me to inadvertently push each other forward through brotherly competition. She knew full well that I would have no desire to read three Primary Phonics books on a Sunday morning. But she also knew that if Kirk had read four, I would be eager to outshine him with five.

As the books got longer, she cut windows in index cards and slid them across the page, allowing me to read one word at a time. It later evolved into sticky-side-up Post-its that I stuck to the tips of my fingers and slid down the page to help ease my tracking issues. With one less distraction, the book came one step closer to actually talking to me.

Mom's greatest skill has always been her ability to find someone at their lowest point, pump them up—with energy, knowledge, and gusto—and push them forward. It's rather magical to witness.

Although this was our normal, it wasn't until I was older that I began to realize how radical so much of this was. Even as she broke away from the institutions of higher learning, she kept the teachings with her. As her colleagues asserted high-level theories at conferences, she was breaking down these concepts so they could be held within the hands and minds of children.

When I look back at the decision she made, I find myself suspended in the tension between extraordinary gratitude and all-encompassing guilt. It's an uncomfortable truth—that the genesis of my learning is based in something that is undeniably unfair. It was unfair for my mom, who had to make an extraordinary sacrifice for us to learn. And it was unfair for our classmates—especially our disabled classmates, who didn't have parents who could make such a sacrifice.

But we needed her intervention. We needed her ability to turn the sparks of interest into the flames of passion. And perhaps there was no time when we needed it more than in middle school.

Afloat

When Kirk hit seventh grade, Mom channeled his energy into building a boat. Not a model boat. Instead, she let him build a fourteen-foot wooden sailboat—in the living room.

He was familiar with the process of building boats. We weren't a family of boaters so much as we were boatbuilders. When I was four and my brother was six, we helped Mom build a tot-sized wooden kayak. "Helping" mostly consisted of twisting copper wire loops that were used to hold the boat together as it was taking form. I can still feel the twinge of the copper pressing a valley into my thumbs as I twisted it over and over and over itself. Mom let Kirk help with sanding and varnishing. My favorite job was to hop inside and paddle the air with a broom as Mom checked the cockpit for size—a job she requested far more frequently than was actually needed.

Half-built boats were a constant throughout our childhood. When we moved to Tulsa, we put our time into a new type of boat. A seventeen-foot rowboat took up residence on the porch. My parents built the frame, but when it came to the hull, they reached outward. Each strip was put in place by a neighbor, a teacher, a friend, or an acquaintance.

They would visit us for a half hour and learn how to add a cedar strip onto the hull, pressing and twisting it into place before stapling it to the inner formwork of the boat. As our network of Tulsa friends and acquaintances expanded, the sides of the boat inched toward closure. We were works in progress. Building community one strip of wood at a time.

The childhood kayak and the community-built rowboat were rather straightforward projects. Kirk's boat was different. Rather than designing the whole thing first, Mom helped Kirk work out a few basics and then began feeding him the same lessons that she had taught her architecture students at RISD. She simplified structural principles and had him feel the differences between materials. He learned to read wood grain and how to work back and forth between structure, materials, and design. All the while, in the middle of our living room, a boat began to emerge.

At the time, I didn't care much for the boat. I found it rather inconvenient. And I wasn't allowed to sit in it. But it brought to life a talent within Kirk that was ignored in the classroom.

The boat would occupy Kirk from middle school to high school. He learned to experiment with a saw and scrap wood, and to make multiple attempts at joinery— the art of attaching two pieces of wood together—until he understood which designs were the strongest. By the time the boat was finished, it had a Plexiglas top so you could see the structure inside of it. And yes, it did float. But more importantly, it propelled him into a passion that allowed his dyslexic mind to thrive. He learned to work with his condition rather than defeat it, and through each step of the process, he redefined learning on his own terms.

Kirk would go on to fall in love with car design.

After he graduated from Princeton, I joked to him that he should move to Paris.

"I've heard Holland is nice," he quipped.

He ended up joining a then-tiny automotive start-up called Rivian, following his inner compass to where his tiny fingers once pointed—westward.

No Such Thing as Later

Around the time that Kirk's boat began to take form on the living room floor, my mom introduced a phrase that she hoped would become the family mantra.

"There's no such thing as later."

The phrase was a rallying cry to combat procrastination. But it was also meant to keep us immersed in the vitality of the present moment. I never fully embraced the phrase—because, let's face it, there is such a thing as later. But we did begin living by its urgency. The phrase provided an antidote for *hurry up and wait*. We weren't going to wait until we were twenty-two to engage with what mattered to us.

As I watched Kirk's boat take shape, I wanted my own project that was real. And there was no such thing as later.

The Times

In the late 2000s, the *New York Times* released a feature on its website that—at the time—felt magical. You could double-click on any word, and a little pop-up with the definition would appear.

My *no-such-thing-as-later* mom gave me a job. I had to read one *New York Times* article per day. But, there was a catch. I only had to read until I encountered a word I didn't understand. Once I had copied the definition into my vocab file, I could stop.

Some days, this meant I only had to read a few words. Faced with Nicholas Kristof's "Two-Thirds of Kids Struggle to Read, and We Know How to Fix It," I would have stopped at word number three: *aphorism*.

But after the glee of a few days of short reads, I began to hang on a little longer. Over time, I forgot about not finishing.

I had discovered that I could ease my tracking problems on screen by highlighting as I read. It was a natural way to keep my place, and no matter how often my eyes switched, I could easily spot where I was.

I was finding that in the short form of an article, I

could accomplish something before my eyes got so tired that I felt the need to quit.

Day by day, article by article, I was building a vocabulary—and a bit of confidence on the side. And with that confidence came a slow but steady introduction to "the real world." I was fascinated by the excitement surrounding our then senator Barack Obama. There was speculation that he would run for president. I wrote a five-paragraph essay about why the A380 was better than the Boeing 787, sparring with Kirk, whose essay argued the opposite. I dug deep into paragraphs about the uncertain future of the war in Iraq. And learned about the mounting concern around climate change.

This was no standardized, predigested, manipulative, carefully fonted, grade-levelized, land-of-make-believe curricular concoction.

I was reading the *New York Times*.

And because Mom had us memorize the countries of the world, when I read the paper, I could store each story on my mental map.

As I slowly made my way through the *Times* each day, my most burning questions were no longer about the words but about the world.

Chocolate

To tell this story ethically, I am going to change the subject that I obsessed over to chocolate. Here's what happened: In middle school, my forays into the *New York Times* had led me to question a subject that shared many parallels with chocolate.

What captured my attention wasn't just the allure of chocolate but the injustice. I had read an article that mentioned child labor practices that sounded, at times, like slavery. I was confused and concerned. How could something that we encounter every day have such a dark history? And how was it that we were all eating up its sweetness while ignoring the injustice at the center of its creation?

I was unsatisfied with my parents' responses to my questioning until they said I could watch a documentary on the subject. This was a big deal. For most of our childhood, my brother and I were not allowed to watch television. We used to chant, "Mom threw the TV down the stairs."

In truth, it was relegated to a box in the basement—its downfall spurred by my mimicking the whiny attitude of D. W. from the TV show *Arthur*.

But we didn't miss it. Kirk and I spent much of our time outside. And the TV would occasionally make its way up the stairs. Usually once per year, for the Super Bowl. Or the day that a half-off VHS tape of *Shrek* was discovered in the clearance bin at the grocery store. Dad sometimes bent the family rules.

The lack of TV meant that Kirk and I weren't used to being inundated by the advertisements and attention-grabbing manipulations of TV land. We weren't used to the urgency of "Offer Ends Soon" or "Supplies Are Limited." We weren't accustomed to the visceral manipulation evoked by the combination of voice, music, and flashy visuals.

As I sat down on the living room couch to watch the chocolate film, I was experiencing something new. I had never seen an investigative documentary.

Played at a reasonable volume from the confines of a small television, the film was sure to be an easy watch. But what I saw was not.

The documentary covered the expected facts: that chocolate comes from cacao beans, which are harvested on farms, usually on the western shores of Africa in Côte d'Ivoire. Many of these farms are deep within the jungle where cacao beans are grown illegally in protected forests.

But rather than just providing an overview of the situation, this documentary brought us there. It followed children to a bus stop on the border of Côte d'Ivoire and Mali. It was here where children, many from poor, rural families in the neighboring countries of Mali and Burkina Faso, were rounded up by traffickers. They were promised they could earn life-changing wages. Some of these children were sent by their families. Others were conned and kidnapped. The film took us on a motorbike down a back road where children were zipped across the border into Côte d'Ivoire. I was haunted by footage of a child, a few years younger than myself, crying out for his parents.

Many of these children were sold to farmers, who forced them to complete excruciating manual labor. During the growing season, the children sprayed pesticides without masks or protection. At harvest time, they used machetes to gather and cut open the cacao beans, emptying the white goo into banana leaves. The beans were dried in the sun until they turned a deep brown. Many of the children worked for over a decade before earning a cent. Those who tried to escape were beaten.

The documentary tracked the supply chain, following cacao beans from rural farms to port cities in Côte d'Ivoire, where the beans are sold to major suppliers before they are shipped to Europe and the United States, where they are processed and made into chocolate delights.

The injustice was alarming. The use of hidden cameras and suspenseful music brought urgency to the crisis. The harrowing cries of a child who had just been kidnapped stood in stark contrast to the cool cadence of a finely suited European executive, defending the actions of his multibillion-dollar corporation.

The documentary accomplished all the things that reading was supposed to. It captured my imagination. And brought me to a place I had never been. It sparked a physical reaction. I was repulsed and horrified. And it became permanently stationed in my mind.

How could it be that something that was consumed at my school every day could have such a dark history? Why did none of us know about this? And why were we doing so much pretend—trying to melt chocolate for s'mores with our environmentally mindful solar ovens without ever mentioning the devastating injustice behind the candy we were consuming with such joy?

I decided that I wanted to make my own documentary. And I wanted it to be about chocolate.

Choc-Doc

The timing of my interest in the chocolate documentary was particularly relevant. In 2001, the world's largest chocolate producers had signed what was called the Harkin-Engel Protocol. It was a promise—by 2005, and later extended to 2008—they would eliminate the worst forms of child slavery from chocolate production. The year 2008 had arrived, but a question lingered—had they?

I began by interviewing a family friend who knew about the politics of chocolate. My mistakes were rampant. I sat her down in front of the blaring light of an open window, stacked the family camcorder on a pile of books, and, after posing a question, pressed Record and declared "Action!"

Eventually, I scrapped the interview, but I still wanted to make the documentary.

So I began researching. And writing. I was drawn to documentary because it was all the things that books weren't. There were no words that jumped around on the page. In fact, there was no page. And yet, through the act of creating a documentary, I would have to do all the things I had been avoiding.

I paced my way through long-form articles and scoured the web for interviews. I wrote a script. And although teachers and friends pressured me to find someone with a British accent to record the voiceover, I settled on narrating the film myself. I would record straight into the built-in mic on the family's PC. I had no cables or proper recording equipment. I just slapped the space bar, raised my voice, and started to read.

"The cacao bean is grown along the western shores of Africa." I looked up at the screen and tapped the space bar. The recording stopped.

"Should we listen to it?" my mom asked.

"No, it was good," I assured her.

"But don't you want to check and see how it sounds?"

I ignored her.

"I would be curious to hear it."

Mom is good at these. Nonthreatening asks. It wasn't an accusation but an invitation. A curiosity.

I moved the playhead to the beginning of the clip and slapped the space bar.

"Ow bean is grown in the—"

I had pressed Record at the same time that I'd begun speaking, and the computer's delay had cut off the opening word of the narration. The recording sounded as if someone had been pinching my nose while I was reading the text.

Take two.

Space bar.

Pause.

"The cacao bean is farmed—"

ERNNRNRNNRNRNNNHHMVVMVMMVM.

The windows started to vibrate. Even though it was early spring, our neighbor had decided to whip out the leaf blower.

I waited. Not sure what to do. Dust and a few sticks tumbled down the driveway with his every swipe.

I was ten minutes in, and I hadn't properly recorded a single sentence. It was as if I was in first grade again, reading at a pace that was choppy and disjointed and frustrating.

Eventually the buzzing began to fade, and so I slapped the space bar.

Deep breath.

Take three.

Quiet

Film is often seen as a place for big egos. There are award galas, red carpets, and magazine covers. On the surface, the industry appears to be a magnet for self-obsession. But I was coming to learn that there is another side of it—technical and dedicated to the craft—that is incredibly humble. A side that dresses in black to make itself invisible, so that all the oxygen of the moment can be given to the story.

On some level, all these little details and technical aspects of the filmmaking processes seemed unimportant—especially when compared with the subject at hand. Why care about the microphone, or the leaf blower, or the number of pixels in a photograph, when those whose stories I was highlighting were facing such greater difficulties?

I was also beginning to feel uncomfortable about telling this story altogether. Was I—sitting in the comfort of my family's home, thousands of miles away—really the right person to be telling this?

Some would argue that I wasn't. But no matter what story I had picked as my first story, I would have come across a similar question. There are uncomfortable power dynamics within every true story—even the ones that we tell about ourselves. To be a documentarian is to be constantly aware of and self-conscious about one's own positioning. And although these questions can make you uncomfortable, they can also make you better at your job. They push you to be more intentional with your every move, more careful with your wording. And more precise with your movement. Sitting with this discomfort isn't just necessary, it's healthy. And rather than ignored, it's best when embraced.

As I continued narrating, searching for images, and finding music, I began to appreciate that these seemingly inconsequential questions of form and documentary process *did* matter.

That I could pay attention to these details is precisely why I should. Although I was just a sixth grader, I had access to something that those whose stories I was highlighting did not: the chocolate consumer.

I was learning that making a story watchable by putting time and attention into how it is presented is precisely how you show respect to those on screen.

Even an invisible hand gesture, which won't show in the film but will change the narrator's intonation, may require seventeen re-recordings. This attention to detail—and willingness to care—is how you make yourself worthy of being trusted to carry one of the most valuable things a human has: their story.

The People Train

When you're behind in school, catching up can be as daunting as it is mundane. But it comes with a gift. It leads you to develop an extraordinary tolerance for tedium, not to mention a gusto for grit.

By the time I reached high school, I had mostly caught up to my peers. That's not to say that my ability to read was entirely fixed. But I was learning to adapt. I also benefited from a radical change in technology. In elementary school, books on tape were large and clunky, and drew attention to themselves. I associated them with long car rides to Grandmother's house, when I felt a deep pit of motion sickness in my stomach.

But suddenly, audiobooks were seamless, playable from one's phone. They allowed me to follow along in the physical book. And when I needed to give my eyes a rest from tracking the jumping text on the page, I could look up without having to stop listening. If I spaced out, I could just pause and replay.

I became so used to working with catch-up intensity that once I was caught up, intensity was all I knew. I didn't think to slow down.

Whenever I could, I kept digging into the latest research on chocolate. The middle school documentary had given me motivation. It didn't change the outcome of the Harkin-Engel Protocol. It didn't change the fact that to this day there are children in the chocolate trade.

But the film did have an impact on those who watched it. At screenings to family friends and again at my school, I would turn back and see tears welling in eyes and slowly sneaking down faces. It was the first time that something I created had a physical impact on another human. As the film ended, many expressed their shock at an issue they didn't even know existed, and several vowed to pay more attention to labeling. But I wanted it to go further.

I used school to dig deeper, quietly commandeering individual assignments to put together the pieces of a much larger puzzle. School offered something that I needed—deadlines. With my sights pinned on remastering the chocolate documentary, I could use teachers' expectations to my advantage. I was honing my skills, using a project on Shakespeare to practice video editing, and a social studies essay to dig deeper into child labor.

I wanted to make this documentary real. I was particularly interested in adding firsthand interviews, so I hijacked two days of a family spring-break trip to interview experts at a nonprofit.

Initially, I thought that nonprofits would be an ideal starting point for documentary work. They have boots on the ground. They want people to care. They are trying to get the word out. And frequently, nonprofits use documentaries to further their cause. I thought that as a filmmaker, a nonprofit would be my best friend.

But as I sat down behind the camera in a warehouse turned office building, I found myself struggling to get those in front of the camera to speak candidly. They clammed up as if they were held hostage by the camera's lens. They could speak to broad-level issues that were easily agreed upon. They could rattle off their organization's mission. They mentioned the importance of eating ethically sourced chocolate. But when it came down to exactly who needed to be held accountable, the responses were meandering and unclear: vague terms that masked meaning and lacked humanity.

I interviewed the program director, then her assistant, and then I was handed over to the development staff. By this time, the interviews had wandered far away from the subject at hand.

"At our winter gala, we hire three local chefs. There are champagne towers. We bring in crystal chandeliers and Chiavari chairs."

It was kind of them to allow me to stick around for an entire day, but I was not here to collect vivid descriptions of floral arrangements at fundraising dinners. In retrospect, perhaps I should have been able to predict the course of this conversation just by looking at the nonprofit's website. I have a rule of thumb that I have found to be ironically reliable: The worse the website, the more insightful an interview. This organization was image-conscious and careful with its words. They had funders to satisfy. I had the wrong people in front of the camera.

Un-planning

In one of the interviews, an employee mentioned a
local shopkeeper who had been forced into the chocolate
trade as a child. I asked if we could visit his shop. She
agreed, hoping that I would purchase some souvenirs to
support the family.

I entered, feigning interest in trinkets but stealing
glances at the shopkeeper when I could. My well-
intentioned guide from the nonprofit shuffled me from
shelf to shelf, flipping through bags and T-shirts with
nonstop chatter, encouraging me to load up on purchases.
After waving stationery at me, she grew bored with my
hesitancy and wandered off. I shyly meandered toward
the counter, where a man, likely in his sixties, sat quietly.
This was him. But I had no idea how to approach him.
I didn't know if he would want to talk with me. Or how
he would react to a boy's questions about his life. But his
personal photographs were pinned to a bulletin board
behind the counter. It seemed he was open on some level.
And so, eventually, I just leaned in and quietly asked, "Can
you tell me your story?"

He was surprised by the odd request. But I would guess that my youthfulness played in my favor.

"Which story?" He smiled. His tone was warm and friendly. He had a grandfatherly quality.

"About coming to America."

Then he began.

He told me about being a young boy, living in a remote community. About how two individuals had come by his house, hoping to steal him. How he and his brother had hidden in a sack. Eventually making his way out of Burkina Faso and into Côte d'Ivoire, how he had been forced to work on cacao farms. He had then escaped and made his way to the United States. At first, he was completely alone. And it took years to rebuild his life in the States.

By the time he finished, my eyes were welling up. The entire morning didn't matter. It was here, in the eyes of someone who had actually experienced the cruelty of this hidden horror, that the dark secrets of chocolate could be understood. Through the window of his eyes, the chocolate trade was humanized.

The People Train

I returned to the shop later that day with my mom, brother, camera, and his permission to record his retelling of his story. He was excited that someone my age was interested.

The interview formed the basis of my renewed chocolate documentary. I spent the next two years scouting and listening, interviewing just shy of fifty people who were in some way connected to the production and trading of chocolate. Some interviews were soul riveting, others about as successful as the conversation about Chiavari chairs. But the act of getting out there, into the realm of the real, taught me about trust and the complexity of truth. It taught me how our understanding is transformed not merely by statistics and analysis, but by memories and stories. And that your telling of a story is only as strong as your connection to those who have experienced it firsthand.

CDS? CVS? CDC?

As I reached the end of high school, I had my sights set on Duke. I wasn't particularly drawn to the basketball or the reputation. Instead, my sights were set on a converted house on the corner of campus—the Center for Documentary Studies.

It's a part of Duke that many students don't even know exists, hidden behind a stretch of trees, perched between a train track and a highway—its acronym confused all too often with the drugstore.

The building is antithetical to everything Duke. At a time when Big Duke was investing millions in spiffing up dining halls, dorms, and libraries, CDS offered something that felt more real. It was here where the chairs squeaked, the floors creaked, where the touch of the human hand was ever present and ever past.

And it was here where I would spend the next four years of my life, living and breathing the documentary process. I learned the technical, often teaching myself with YouTube tutorials, until it became second nature to make sure that my audio levels were between −24 and −12 decibels. Or that my ISO, aperture, and shutter speed—three ways of controlling how a camera processes light—were in balance. And I made a point of meeting one-on-one with every instructor I ever had.

It was through documentary that I found myself witnessing the joy of a sixth grader finishing her first violin solo. And the excitement on an eleven-year-old's face, removing his helmet after welding for the first time.

I interviewed a grandmother from Durham, who described the unending frustration of watching the city's predominantly Black neighborhood become fragmented by highways, housing prices, and gentrification. And spoke to an Indonesian environmentalist who had witnessed his backyard bulldozed and burned by palm oil plantations. Through a glitchy Skype interview, he described his life's mission—to save local wildlife. I learned to question more intentionally, write more pointedly, and photograph more carefully.

Documentary allows you to cut through the small talk. To get right to the heart of another human's being. When you show that you are capable of looking someone in the heart, eye contact becomes less relevant. Behind the camera, asking questions, I never felt that my physical appearance needed fixing.

It wasn't always a smooth ride. Sometimes I got lost. In Louisiana, I found myself on a shrimping boat in the middle of a violent thunderstorm with Donald. We swayed back and forth while listening to the intermittent crackle of voices shouting in French over the radio. The only bit I could make out was the name of a fisherman whose radio had gone dead. "Rodney . . . Rodney . . . Rodney . . . ," his neighbors shouted over the airwaves. Rodney did make it back to shore. And the story—of his community on the front lines of climate change and land loss—was something I would work on for the next several years.

At CDS, I no longer felt the need for my learning to take place in secret. I could be up-front about my intentions. I found assignments that pushed my skill set. And I felt at home. Perhaps it's not surprising, then, that it was here, in this small community, nearly a decade after making my first documentary, that I decided to turn the camera on myself for the first time.

The stares always feel like an interruption. A micro moment that takes you out of your day, out of your rhythm, out of your body. You're headed toward the exit of the college library. A well-known basketball player who made national news last week has just entered the building and is walking straight toward you. You recognize him from a distance. And it almost looks like he recognizes you.

Or, wait.

No.

He's giving you the stare.

For nearly seventy-five feet,

as he walks toward you

and you toward him,

his eyes are locked on your face.

Years' worth of sound bites from Kirk and Dad and teachers and coaches echo in your head.

"Don't let them get to you."

"Suck it up."

"Ignore them."

"Just walk away."

But he's still staring at you.

What do you do?

How do you break the tension?

A head lift?
A nod?

You decide on a nod.
Upward, as if he is someone you know.

Can you break through?
Nope.
He's still staring.

Why does it feel as if your presence is an interruption?
As if you are violating the sanctity of the space?
For a second, you want to lash out.
You want to proclaim:

I know
These eyes are different
and new
and askew.
But I promise
that the experience
of looking at my eyes—
however new or foreign it may
be to you

is nowhere near
as uncomfortable
as being greeted
by the blank stare of your face,
which hasn't yet decided
on disgust
or contempt
or familiarity

and is frozen in limbo.

But
you
don't
say that.

You
don't
say
anything.

You keep
your head
pointed
forward.

And
try
not to
think
about it.

And suck
it up.

And
walk
away.

Dear Starer,

I just wish you knew how deep
our connection could be.

Until Next Time.

The Public Eye

By the time I was a senior in college, I had lost faith in the platitudes we prescribe to those with difference. I no longer believed that this issue was entirely my own.

As I looked toward the future, I sensed that my misaligned eyes could be costly to my career. In school, it was common for teachers or professors to initially find my eyes off-putting, but I always had a semester or so to win them over—time to prove that I was more than meets the eye.

But in the job market, a good first impression is critical. I would have twenty to thirty minutes to seal my fate. I didn't want to discuss my vision in a job interview—I didn't think it was relevant. So I needed a way to push potential employers to get over the discomfort associated with my eyes. I thought about making a video and linking to it in my email signature.

James Robinson
207-XXX-XXXX
What's up with my eyes?

Throughout my childhood, my family had repeatedly asked me to make a video that would allow them to experience my alternating vision. I had never thought it a worthy subject. But now, the stakes were different.

In the disability community, there is a name for what I was doing. This is often referred to as "the disability tax."

The disability tax comes in many forms. One of the most ubiquitous and time-costly is education. Many disabled people are expected to teach the people around them how to adapt to their needs. At first, it might appear reasonable to have disabled people advocate for their needs. But in practice, it's exhausting.

By making a video, I was trying to pay my disability tax up front. I would have to explain my eyes only once, and the conversation would be over. My hope was that acquaintances and potential employers could get over their discomfort, and we could move on. Video seemed like a way to save time.

Up Against

As I began to make the video, I realized there was a wrinkle. I had always thought that the starers were staring because they had never seen eyes like my own. But I was up against more than just unfamiliarity. The truth is, misaligned eyes are ubiquitous within pop culture. In fact, they've long been a source of Hollywood fascination.

Filmmakers need shorthand. They need visual cues to communicate the essence of a character's being at a glance. And in Hollywood, misaligned eyes became shorthand for characters who are disconnected from reality. What better way to show a disconnect than by altering the way that we all connect—through the eyes?

The use of strabismus to connote danger, fear, and alien-like behavior has been around since the inception of the film industry. In the first half of the twentieth century, actors with strabismus played the roles of murderers and pedophiles, adding fear-inducing mystique to their characters.

Take a look at three of the biggest blockbuster films from my childhood.

In *The Lion King*, as Scar, the antagonist, leads a murderous rebellion, he is surrounded by his compatriots—evil hyenas whose eyes meander out of alignment as they slobber.

In Harry Potter, Mad-Eye Moody is capable of attacking dark wizards only because he himself is able to think like one. His wandering eye intimidates and entertains, alluding to his connection to the dark side.

In *Men in Black*, an alien inhabits the body of a pawn shop owner. The first suggestion that something is amiss with his humanity—his eyes are misaligned.

The portrayals aren't limited to the cinema hall. Even as television begins to shy away from negative portrayals of disability, strabismus is one of a handful of conditions that is still openly mocked without social consequence.

On *The Late Late Show*, host James Corden pulls a prank on the famous soccer player David Beckham by unveiling a statue of him. The joke is that the statue is intentionally ugly, its body morphed out of proportion with eyes that point outward. The viral video has had nearly 48 million views.

Surprisingly, there are few places where the trope is more present than in animated films targeted toward children. A team of researchers at the University of Colorado conducted a review and found that strabismic characters were twenty-one times more likely to be portrayed as unintelligent than intelligent, three times more likely to be villains than heroes, and nearly five times more likely to be followers than leaders.

Ignore-ance

When I encountered these portrayals, I didn't care. I never thought that they bothered me. In fact, I laughed the first time that I saw the James Corden prank.

I didn't see *The Lion King* until I was in my twenties, but even when I finally did watch it, I didn't go home thinking about the hyenas' eye misalignment.

When I watched *Men in Black* with my family, not one of us thought twice about the scene in which my eyes were portrayed as alien.

But no matter how much I didn't care, I was never going to be immune from the consequences. The impact of the cultural story that we tell ourselves about people with misaligned eyes—that they are unstable, untrustworthy, unintelligent, and unworthy of dignity—extends far beyond the screen.

Science Friction

At the turn of the century, scientists began studying the impact of strabismus—not on those who have it, but instead on those who encounter peers with the condition. Essentially, they began studying the starers. The results were alarming.

They learned that between ages three and four, most children don't even notice eye misalignment. By age five, they describe these eyes as different. And around age six, a negative response emerges.

At that point, children are less likely to want to invite those with misaligned eyes to their birthday parties. By age eight, they're less likely to want to sit next to a classmate with misaligned eyes.

Elementary school teachers were found to perceive students with strabismus as less intelligent, less attentive, and less cute than their normal-eyed peers.

As adults, those with strabismus are perceived as

less attractive and less desirable. Studies have found that employers are less likely to hire those with a noticeable eye misalignment. And that they are seen as less trustworthy and sincere.

This was particularly true for women, and for those whose eyes point inward—sometimes described as "crossed eyes." In fact, numerous studies suggest that those whose eyes point inward face more severe prejudice than those whose eyes point outward.

This prejudice is not something we are born with. Instead, it appears to be taught. It's taught through the stories that we pass down. It's taught in the moments when we cross our eyes, stick out our tongue, and make a face that is "crazy." Perhaps more than anything, it's taught by the multibillion-dollar studios that continue to fall back on an age-old trick, packaging and selling it to a global audience.

Inversion

As I set out to make my video, I didn't know exactly what I wanted to say. My emotions were tangled. But I knew my audience. This video was for all the people who were staring at me.

On some level, I wanted revenge. To force them to consider their own actions. To reveal the indignity of the social mirror. But as I began crafting the film, this urge waned.

My frustration toward the starers was valid. But it wasn't productive. Alienating them wouldn't help anyone. I needed them to be on my side. I wanted them to want to connect with me. And, remember, I wanted them to hire me.

Over time, I began to appreciate the fact that the starers had also been robbed. They had been robbed of the knowledge of how to look at someone with misaligned eyes, and how to interact with them seamlessly. During moments when they could have felt relaxed, many were instead distracted by awkwardness and preoccupied with a feeling of disconnect.

It was the story surrounding such eyes that needed to change. They had seen my eyes attached only to bodies that were cruel, cunning, uninteresting, and alien. My story would have to prove that I could be the opposite— witty, kind, open-minded, forgiving, vulnerable, and undeniably human.

I wasn't looking for remorse. I was seeking connection.

What's in a Name?

Up until that point, the names attached to my condition were used for medical purposes:

There is

Exotropia—when eyes point outward.

Esotropia—when the eyes point inward.

Intermittent—meaning eyes are misaligned sometimes but not all the time.

Alternating—meaning the viewer switches which eye they are looking out of with their central vision.

And my own complication, *anomalous retinal correspondence*.

All of these names fit under the umbrella term *strabismus*.

These names are useful, but they were designed to serve a specific community—the medical community. The terms are crucial when providing treatment or working through scientific papers.

But I wasn't living in a scientific paper. I wasn't living in doctors' offices or on sheets of paper. And the string of names wasn't working for me. It never had.

Whale Eyes

While digging through archival footage, I encountered a clip that suggested that whales see out of one eye at a time. The tape was from the 1970s, its veracity clearly questionable.

But it got me thinking about whales and how I was oddly jealous of them. We love looking at whales. And yet none of us have ever questioned the fact that we can look into only one of their eyes at a time.

It felt as if the whales were afforded the acceptance that I was seeking.

"Whale Eyes." The name rolled off the tongue. It was silly and absurd. But that almost made it feel more appropriate. What I was doing—teaching adults how to make eye contact—seemed equally absurd. Surely I was allowed to have some fun with it.

Whale Eyes stuck in a way that no other name that

was assigned to my eyes had stuck before. Friends and classmates spoke it with more confidence than they did *lazy eye*, although it's true that Ryan's middle-school declaration had provided a name that was familiar.

But Whale Eyes added a layer of love. It's hard to say the name without a smile. And it mattered that the name was casual and playful.

I sensed that many of my peers were afraid to step forward and lean in. They chose not to engage, out of a fear of offending. Whale Eyes freed us from that awkwardness.

As I typed out the letters into a rough draft of a script, I could feel a sense of inversion on the page. For so much of my life, my eyes were at war with words. This time, the words were setting my eyes free. They were forming a bridge between the public eye and my own.

With a renewed sense of purpose, I set out to create the film.

To Release Is to Let Go

On so many mornings, as I pushed myself through the difficulties of reading, I would open the home page of the *New York Times* and search for an article of interest.

But the morning of July 14, 2021, as I followed my ingrained routine, I was met with something familiar. My own eyes were staring back at me—alternating back and forth on the home page of the newspaper that had taught me how to read.

Above the cinemagraph was a headline:

How Life Looks Through My 'Whale Eyes'

INTERMISSION

Take a break from the book
and watch the twelve-minute film:

whaleeyes.org/watch

Whale Watching

I was living in Los Angeles, working as an assistant to a pair of documentary filmmakers. I had set my alarm for six a.m., thinking that I would take a few screenshots and have an hour before work to take in the moment. But around four thirty a.m., my phone began buzzing at random intervals. Despite my attempts to silence it, the buzzing would not stop.

It wasn't a rogue alarm. Rather, I was receiving email after email. As the East Coast woke up and sipped their coffee, they, too, were checking the news. And perhaps out of the luck of a slow news day, hundreds of thousands of them were clicking on the same pair of severely misaligned eyes. They weren't just watching. They were responding.

I am crying and shaking and trying to figure out how to share your video with friends and family.

It's like having someone scratch an itch you didn't know you had, in the deepest part of your soul.

I sat perched between Rinchen, my girlfriend, and Kirk as we Zoomed with the rest of our family back in Maine. Together, we sifted through the onslaught of comments.

That we had made it to this point at all was surprising. A year earlier, in my final semester of college, I had worked on a twenty-four-minute version of the film, made on a shoestring budget, mostly with borrowed equipment. When COVID hit and my senior year was cut short, I finished the film from home, using my iPhone and incorporating the fifty-pound bag of popcorn that my mom had bought in anticipation of lockdown.

After graduating from college on the living room couch, I faced an uncertain future. COVID had knocked out my prior plans. So I spent the next nine months frantically searching for a job.

A cold email in September, with several follow-ups in November, led to a surprise call in January. Adam Ellick, the head of Opinion Video at the *Times*, had seen a film that I made about climate change and was intrigued. I thought he was calling because he needed someone to transcribe interviews, or sift through raw footage. But Adam wanted to pick up *Whale Eyes*, condense it to ten minutes, and publish it.

I agreed, swallowing the fact that I had just started work as a production assistant a few days earlier. For the next few months, I spent nights and weekends trimming and sharpening the film. I developed the metaphor of the USS *Normal* and the Sea of Difference to describe the isolation that often accompanies Whale Eyes. I turned my bedroom into a film studio, tilting the mattress up against the window to block out the light. The room was small, but with my camera pressed against the wall, I could just barely film a shot of my full body—as long as I took my shoes off.

Working with Adam, I found what most filmmakers dream of—precise and brutal critique, paired with near total creative freedom. It felt like there was only one rule: I had to use their fonts.

Now, several months after I had begun refining *Whale Eyes* with the team at the *Times*, the little video that could was steaming ahead into the hands of those who had eyes like my own.

Finally, it was not about me—but us. Through tweets, comments, and emails, we let out a sigh. A deep breath long held within. A collective release.

There was Paige, a ten-year-old in New Zealand, who

watched the film and was inspired to give a speech to her entire school about the years of bullying she had faced from students and teachers alike.

And Hannah, who had also been to vision therapy and would go on to memorize the entire script, reciting it in a speech competition.

There was Jordan, who was born blind in one eye and knew what it meant to strike out in T-ball.

And Karen, a journalist, who had been told she would not be able to appear on television so long as she had misaligned eyes.

Neil, a rabbi in Boston, was walking with a friend and trying to explain how his eyes are different when the friend turned and said, "Oh, you have Whale Eyes?" It was the first time someone in his inner circle had understood what he was seeing.

To release is to let go. And with the release of the video came the shared outpouring of pent-up emotions and stories. From the part of our body that we most associated with isolation, we were feeling a sense of community.

I heard from teachers I had lost contact with and many more I had never met. From old friends and colleagues. And, overwhelmingly, from an emerging community of fellow whales.

It felt as if every bit of compassion that had ever been withheld because of my eyes was fire-hosed my way on one morning in the middle of July. I was teary-eyed, overwhelmed, and very late for work.

I used to be afraid of the word *disabled.* I thought it wasn't mine to say. That I wasn't disabled enough to use it.

I wasn't alone in my avoidance. Growing up, I heard a myriad of substitutions. *Differently abled* and *otherly abled. Special needs. Special education. Special eyes.*

I heard friends, parents, and teachers dance around the word *disability,* as if it secretly meant something sinister. As if its hidden definition was weakness.

But what I didn't understand until my twenties is that for decades, the disability community has been fighting for this word to mean something else—not weakness but protection.

In other areas of our culture, we don't conflate these two ideas.

When we see an advertisement for *Sunday Night Football* with a player who is covered head to toe in shoulder pads, helmet, mouth guard, thigh pads, and cleats as he growls at the camera, nobody is thinking "weak."

When we see an image of a firefighter, with turnout gear and a breathing apparatus, we think "heroic," not "weak."

When we see the construction worker, in a high-visibility vest and hard hat, we think "safety," not "weakness."

People use protection because they are in a situation that is potentially harmful—not because they are weak. For decades, disabled Americans have found themselves to be in danger. They're in danger of neglect and abuse: Disabled people are four times more likely to be the victim of a violent crime. At the workplace, they're in danger of being wrongfully terminated. At school, they're in danger of exclusion.

As a result, the disability community came together and, in the 1970s—riding on the coattails of the civil rights movement—demanded that the federal government ratify legislation that would provide them protection.

They were told that they were a burden. That the US economy would decline if their reentry into society was funded. But they persisted.

They held protests at federal offices. From Washington, DC, to New York. Chicago to Los Angeles. Seattle to Philadelphia. The demonstrations came to a head in San Francisco, where protesters held a sit-in that lasted twenty-five days. They garnered support from trade unions, nonprofits, and even the employees of the federal building they were occupying. Rallied by their member Brad Lomax, the Black Panthers documented the sit-ins and provided hot meals to occupiers.

Together, they demanded that Section 504 be ratified. In the decades that followed, the community continued its struggle, leading to the passage of a series of bills that would transform the disability experience for millions of Americans.

With minimal funds, the disability community led one of the most successful civil rights campaigns in human history. And they fought for a definition of disability that was broad and inclusive:

"A physical or mental impairment that substantially limits one or more major life activities."

That includes learning. And reading.

I was a child with a 504 plan. It was because of the disability rights movement that the school was legally required to provide me the accommodations that I needed. It turned out, the very same community that I had been ashamed to admit my connection to had been fighting for me.

Of course, it wasn't always perfect. Sometimes the walk to the extra-time room was drenched in shame. Some classmates felt that I was being given an unfair advantage.

Some teachers acted as if they were doing me a favor, rather than fulfilling a legal obligation. Others were fierce advocates for my learning.

Looking back, if I could change one thing about my childhood, it wouldn't be the failed surgeries or the hours spent holding a string to my nose, or the difficulty I had learning to read. Instead, I wish someone had told me what that word *disabled* really meant.

To tell a child that they are disabled is to tell them that they are protected. That long before they took their first breath, there was a community that was fighting for them. It's a community that continues to fight to this day.

And rather than subscribe to a definition of *weakness*, or come up with alternative words that ignore this history—rather than have them take the same test six times so they can avoid the shame associated with the extra-time room—I hope that today's children can experience what I felt when I mentioned to a disabled scholar that it had taken me two decades to accept that I was part of the disability community.

Reaching out her hand, she heartily declared, "Welcome."

Getting People to Care

Whale Eyes was built on the faith that our vision is transferable. That you can borrow my eyes and connect with me through my vision. And that for a few moments, we can become each other.

In the weeks after the film was released, I felt a transformation in my relationships. I saw my friends, family, neighbors, and even my landlord, kindly and quietly look back into the eye that was looking at them. Instead of awkwardness, I was met with something gentle—their ability and willingness to care.

It wasn't just that they had seen through my eyes. It was that they had seen themselves through my eyes. And that glimpse had led them to change.

The film clarified my own vision—I quit my job to

embark as a freelancer, motivated by the lesson that the primary job of the documentarian is to get people to care.

It's a job that I believe we share.

Perhaps you don't think of yourself as a filmmaker or a documentarian or a writer or a poet. But if you've written a text, or posted a video, or taken a photograph, then I would argue that you've at least dabbled. And regardless of the path you pursue, at some point in your life, it will become your responsibility—and your duty—to entice the world into caring.

So if the first part of this book was about my eyes, then the second—and more exciting part—is about yours. Because I want to see through your eyes. And hear through your ears. And experience the magic of writing, where your inner voice can become my inner voice.

The Job of Caring

Caring is the precursor to action. The precursor to policy. It can drive movements and marches. It can transform relationships. Of course, none of these results are guaranteed, but without the ability to get others to care, not much can happen.

I truly believe that getting someone to care is one of the most profound things you can do in your time on this earth. And yet, it can be misleading. And tricky. The confusion often begins with that word: *getting*.

Getting People to Care

"Getting someone to care" sounds like we should be receiving something. Like we are owed. And certainly, in some cases, maybe it does feel like people owe something. I certainly felt I was owed eye contact.

But *getting* someone to care is really an act of *giving*.

It's an act of giving a story and a set of tools that will convince your audience to hold something that is delicate close to their chest.

So here is my offering—five tools that have taught me how to transform perception and get someone to care in the digital age.

Precise Moment

When I was in college, one of my closest friends flung the door open, hopped onto my bed, and shouted, "HOW IS MOM DOING?"

Mom.

Not "How is *your* mom doing?"

Not "How is *my* mom doing?"

Just Mom.

If you've ever met Haffa, then you know that this is in character. Sudden spurts of exuberant joy, often unannounced. He's a man of big surprise entries.

Our friendship is unlikely—and in many ways we couldn't be more unalike. I grew up in a stable family, the son of two college-educated parents. Haffa grew up in a family of herders, raised by his mom, who never went to school.

Haffa is joyous, unassuming, and completely unafraid of deadlines. He's up close and personal. At one point he turned to me and said, "You are like the papa, I am like the puppy."

Haffa has a distinct definition of friendship: "It's when what's mine is yours and what's yours is mine."

Our friendship is a cultural exchange. Sometimes we need each other. Most of the time, though, we find joy in social and cultural sparring, competitively jabbing at each other's cultural quirks.

And because home was far away, on holidays and weekends, we spent our downtime together.

"I feel like a peacock," he declared while waddling in excitement as we visited a beach in Maine.

His declaration of "Mom" was part of this cultural exchange. He was, indeed, asking about my mom. But in his home community, you don't use an article like "*my* mom" or "*your* mom." Instead, even when talking about a friend's parent, you just say "Mom."

His question was a direct translation. But there was more to it than that. Among his American friends, it was only my mom who lost the possessive article before her name. He wasn't saying, this is how we do it in my home community; he was saying, I respect your mom as if she were my own.

I will always remember the precise moment: his joyous question, the hop onto the bed, the your-space-is-my-space-and-my-space-is-your-space. On that day, my mom became his mom and his mom became my mom. Through a dropped possessive pronoun, he had declared that we were brothers.

Keep It Precise

Documentarians have an issue. There is simply too much to care about. How do you slim the world down? How do you give someone a gift that they can actually carry with them? How do you make caring portable?

The entirety of my complicated friendship with Haffa is too massive and unpredictable to let someone carry. But I can give you a moment—a dropped pronoun that is less than a centimeter on a printed page, yet holds our miles-wide friendship and our brotherhood.

Whale Eyes is about something even smaller than that. It's about the ten seconds when you're meeting me for the first time. And you're trying to figure out which eye to look into. And you feel yourself start to get uncomfortable and unsure of how to look at my face. And precisely at the moment when we're supposed to be coming together and connecting, both of us feel this magnetic force that is pushing us apart.

Every element in the film is aligned with what you need to know when you are confused in that moment: Why my eyes alternate back and forth. Why I might miss your hand when I go to shake it. What can happen to us when we try to ignore this. Why it's still worth leaning in. And how you can overcome the momentary discomfort—by looking back into the eye that is looking at you.

The best moments are fleeting. And the most precise objects can fit within your hand. A glass bead from a broken necklace. A smirk. Or a three-prong fork. These are your telescopes. Tiny moments that slyly encompass the entirety of an issue.

Your goal is to find such a bead and make your audience care about it. But within that bead is the reflection of something much more curious, intriguing, and vast.

Finding Precision

Finding these moments can be counterintuitive. But the things that we care about the most—the things we are most proud of, and the things that we hold close to our sense of who we are—aren't always the things that we are best prepared to make other people care about.

Oftentimes, as storytellers, we do better when we talk about the things that to us might appear entirely unremarkable but to others stick out as odd or mysterious: the last piece of a jigsaw puzzle that somehow doesn't fit.

So how do you find precise moments that are worth paying attention to? How do you say, *Yes, this is it. This is what I am looking for. This is a perception that I can change.* How do you identify the things that you are especially positioned to make the world care about?

It helps to be on the lookout for a very specific emotion.

When the term you're
looking for doesn't exist,

invent it.

Out-Trigue

N.

A peculiar emotion that is experienced when your cultural boundary is pierced. A hint of confusion, often accompanied by a dollop of fear, a sprinkling of embarrassment, or a subdued giggle. Your expectations have been violated, and yet on some level, you are curious.

You'll experience out-trigue when someone stands way too close in an empty room . . .

. . . or if you're stuck in a flash mob . . .

You'll experience out-trigue if you look at a map of flight

paths, and in a sea of straight lines,

there is one aircraft that seems to be wandering out of

position, round and round in circles,

aimlessly meandering.

Out-Trigue

The first time I spoke with Paul Kram, a retired software engineer from Massachusetts, he told me a story that encapsulates out-trigue.

Years earlier, he had flown to Colorado to visit his cousin Rois (pronounced Rose). The two are close. Paul considers her one of the most important people in his life. And it had been nearly a year since they had seen each other. Rois had exciting news. She was pregnant with her first child.

On the night that he arrived, Rois invited Paul to dinner with her husband and mother-in-law. But things got funky when Paul arrived at the house.

He knocked on the door, and an older woman, probably in her sixties, answered. "I figured that was her mother-in-law," Paul recalled.

But as Paul walked into the kitchen, there was another woman. Someone he had never seen before. She was about six feet tall and had her hair pulled up in a bun, and coincidentally, she, too, was pregnant.

"I figured that was a friend of Rois's who also happens to be pregnant—they have a lot in common."

Paul hadn't been told about the surprise guest, but the dinner was casual, and so he did what anyone would do when encountering an unexpected stranger at a dinner party. He walked across the room, extended his hand, and said, "Hi, I'm Rois's cousin Paul."

There was a pause. An awkward pause. Then, the woman chuckled. "Hi, Rois's cousin Paul, I'm Rois."

The room devolved into laughter. Out-trigue dissolved. But there was more to this moment than a playful prank between two close cousins.

In truth, Paul had just put one of his most closely held secrets on full display.

Proso

With his botched introduction, Paul inadvertently unveiled a medical condition for which he had gotten a diagnosis years earlier. It's a condition that is particularly hard to explain, leading Paul—and many others—to hide it.

Paul has *prosopagnosia*, or face blindness, meaning he has difficulty recognizing people, including his closest friends and family. In moments when he flubs, Paul's condition invokes out-trigue. And not in a good way.

"People can think you're a jerk when you see them every day and don't even say hi."

The thing is, on the few occasions when Paul disclosed his condition in an attempt to ease the awkwardness, he found it only made the situation worse. When he told coworkers and neighbors that he was face blind, nearly everyone tried to wiggle out of their discomfort, replying, "Oh, I'm bad with names, too."

It's a phrase that those with face blindness have come to bemoan. On the surface, it's a well-intentioned response. But it's also a roadblock. It undermines Paul's ability to explain himself—and how he needs others to adapt to his condition.

So Paul did what many with prosopagnosia have done. He stopped trying to explain his condition and kept it a well-guarded secret.

Keeping proso a secret isn't just inconvenient; it can be devastating. Proso had significantly shaped Paul's life, limiting the environments in which he felt comfortable to small-group settings. It had steered him away from gatherings and parties, in which he would see familiar faces outside of their usual context. And it had left many people with an odd and inaccurate impression of him— seemingly aloof or uncaring.

"It's a hard thing for people to understand. They are bewildered. They have to trust you to believe that this is real."

Out-Trigue

The thing about out-trigue is that it pushes you in two directions. In moments of out-trigue, you find yourself "-trigued." Fully captivated by an unexpected oddity. But rather than being drawn into a connection through *intrigue*, you find yourself leaning out, as your cultural anchor pulls you away from the reality you've just experienced. Perhaps you begin laughing, blushing, or at the very least, questioning.

Oftentimes—as Paul so frequently experienced—out-trigue fades into an awkward and insecure silence.

But it doesn't have to. When you experience out-trigue, the key is to kindly and quietly lean in. It's during these micro moments of misunderstanding when we are most ripe to connect with each other. It's easier said than done: Transforming out-trigue into connection often requires extraordinary trust.

Leaning In

When I met Paul, there were only six people on the planet who knew he had this condition. I was number seven. And I was about to ask him if he wanted to make that number much, much larger.

The *Times* had asked me to make three more videos about people with difficult-to-explain conditions.

Paul's story seemed particularly ripe: A tweak in the viewer's reaction to his condition could quickly turn their out-trigue into connection.

Paul needed to challenge the cultural process of recognition. He didn't want his friends and coworkers to reintroduce themselves at every head turn. Rather, he needed the ability to ask, "Could you remind me who you are?" without it being a big deal. He needed a reintroduction that was seamless.

A video would leave Paul with a tool that he could show others. It would also allow him to help a silent and fragmented community of people with the condition, including those who might learn through the video that they themselves are face blind.

Though Paul and I don't have a whole lot in common, our experience with out-trigue brought us together, forming the basis for our mutual trust. I, too, knew what it meant to light this peculiar emotion in others. Through our shared experiences on the wrong side of out-trigue, Paul and I connected.

Social Circling

In the calls leading up to our meeting, Paul and I had chatted not only about the details of face blindness, but also about his passion for flying. Paul is an avid glider pilot, and he was excited to show me one of his favorite places on earth—the airstrip of the Sugarbush Soaring Association.

It is here where he is towed in a glider thousands of feet into the air and then released: left alone to maneuver his engineless aircraft in a careful dance with the wind. It is here where he loves to stay afloat in the thin air for hours at a time, circling over the same spot—over and over and over again—as he uses the upward lift of thermal columns to gain altitude.

In a sky full of motored planes flying in straight lines, the path of a glider would likely inspire out-trigue. It's only when you learn that it's been flying without an engine that you can appreciate the ingenuity of a glider's path.

As we spoke about how Paul navigated social situations, I saw a similar ingenuity in his social strategies. Like the plane, his every move was calculated to keep him afloat.

Paul creates a mental checklist, noting unique behaviors and physical traits that can help him identify coworkers, friends, and relatives. The characteristics can be incredibly detailed. One friend has a polyp the size of a sesame seed in the white of his left eye. For most, it would go unnoticed. But for Paul, it's like a name tag.

Paul identifies people by the way they walk, the sound of their voice, their posture, and their eye color. Other features—clothing, hair, and jewelry—are less reliable.

Paul has become an expert in recognizing people through their secondary features. But the strategy is incredibly draining, and it isn't fail-safe. For example, Rois was pregnant, so her posture had changed. And she hadn't yet said anything when he walked into the room, depriving Paul of yet another identifying clue, leaving him primed to whiff.

Fast-Forward

I met Paul in person for the first time the evening before we were to film his interview. I had come to Vermont straight from New York City, where I had been filming an interview for another piece in the series. The change of pace—to a deserted ski resort where the cinematographer and I were the sole guests—was unnerving.

Paul and I had been moving quickly, both of us. We had connected just two weeks before the flying season was to end. Now, in the final week, the weather and wind patterns were unpredictable. It was anyone's guess as to whether Paul would be able to fly for the shoot the following day.

Standing in the moonlit stillness of the airstrip, the speed with which we were exposing Paul's situation seemed impulsive. It was a life-changing decision, from which there would be no point of return. And yet, exposing the secrets of a sprightly, quick-witted, and highly likable man still seemed like the right thing to do. We had come through a lot to get to this point: together, through hours of shared conversation, and separately, in our parallel decisions to go public with our stories.

Paul was placing an extraordinary amount of trust in my filmmaking. After the interview, he would have no input into my output, leaving him in a vulnerable position. Because this film was for the *Times*, he wouldn't get to see it before it was published. And he wasn't just trusting me with a few minutes of film; he was trusting me with one of the most sensitive aspects of his life.

Circling

Over several months of editing—punctuated by weeks spent yelling at the glitchiest project file I have ever worked with—I assembled Paul's story into video form. Using interactive experiments, Paul's interview, archival clips, and animation, my goal was to push viewers past out-trigue and guide them toward connection.

I felt indebted to Paul. Responsible for his trust as much as I was grateful for it. Through our film, Paul was inverting his relationship with face blindness—allowing his secret to be broadcast in one of the most public forums society has to offer. This would be the first time that many of his own friends would hear of his experience with a condition that he had long attempted to outmaneuver.

I called him the night before we premiered his film. He seemed at ease and in good humor, which in some ways surprised me. I was quite nervous for him to watch it.

On the morning we published, he was insistent that his first viewing of the film be uninterrupted—no pauses for buffering, no long waits for the Wi-Fi to catch up. He was still in Vermont, where his internet connection was choppy. So even though the piece was published on NYTimes.com at six in the morning, he decided he was going to wait until one o'clock, when the piece was published on YouTube, because he felt the viewing experience might be smoother.

That meant that he spent the entire morning receiving emails from friends and family who were excited about the film that he had starred in but not yet seen. When one p.m. rolled around, we were finally able to send him the YouTube link. He watched the film. The full thing, without interruption.

I was squirming in my seat. I knew from the comments that the film was having a hefty impact on those out-trigued by his condition, who were grateful for a pathway to lean in. But Paul's response still caught me by surprise.

"You connected me to myself!" he exclaimed. "That is a precious gift."

Tension

"I've only had one student cry when we do this," Kelly announced as she introduced her surprise activity.

Surely, I am thinking, *it's about to be two.*

My problem with pop quizzes has never been so much with the quiz but with the pop.

It's the spring of my junior year of college, and I have managed to finagle my way into Our Culinary Cultures, the most popular course at the university. It's a food writing class. And while many are there for the promise of the food, I actually showed up for the writing.

Not surprisingly, I found myself in a class of self-described foodies—surrounded by classmates who were experienced with sauces and sausages, noodles and strudels.

I was a prolific napkin folder. Food was something I consumed quickly. As fuel. And the prelude to eating—cooking—was something that I habitually wiggled out of. I showed up to college with the ability to scramble eggs, heat up a frozen pizza, and microwave just about anything, so long as the directions were on the box.

What I had learned in the weeks leading up to this moment was that even my lack of a relationship with food was indeed, a relationship with food. And Kelly would trick me into finding it. Her teaching style was like that of an unconventional boxer. Most professors used repeated jabs: Read-read. Problem-problem. Test-test.

But Kelly got us to relax. We gossiped. She'd get you to let your guard down, and then, at the height of vulnerability, strike the most potent punch you would receive all semester:

"Your work can only be as good as your primary sources." KAPOW: a stealthy stab of truth that forever changed my research habits.

Before handing back our first essays, she playfully announced to the class: "James Robinson, you are never allowed to use the words *simple* or *deep* in your writing ever again."

KAPOW.

What Kelly taught us was that the simple stuff could get you to the deep stuff. That we were holding the complexity of the world on the edge of our fork. We just had to see it. Through our chatty conversation, we could reach a conclusion that was just as raw, human, thought-provoking, and real as the high-level discussions being carried out in classrooms down the hall: classes that we were glad to be missing as we chowed down on spaghetti pizza that Jamie had cooked up the night before.

The Assignment

"You will each fry an egg," Kelly instructed.

Fortunately, she went first. I hovered: Close enough to the back so that I wouldn't be called on to go next. Close enough to the front that I could take rigorous mental notes.

She flicked a small pat of butter onto the pan and drove it around like a Zamboni, with artful gyrations of her wrist.

In one sweeping hand motion, she cracked an egg, emptied it into the pan, and tossed the shell.

The class hushed as the gelatinous ooze clouded into white. All eyes on the pan.

After shaking the egg loose from the bottom, she rocked it back and forth, building momentum until a nonchalant flick sent it flying. The egg arced neatly over the pan and flopped down on center, the 180 completed with a satisfying sizzle.

Oooh. The class let out a collective gasp that was as impressed as it was wary of our imminent venture into culinary acrobatics.

Eyes met as the task was digested.

Two at a time, we took turns. Casual conversations between egg-flipper and audience quieted each time an egg was about to take off.

"I once had a student flip it so high that it hit the ceiling," Kelly exclaimed, raising her eyes to the beams.

The contest was on.

With foodie flamboyance, eggs flew.

Some were cracked single-handedly. Others took a few tries.

I awaited a lull in the action to slip in my turn. I wanted to avoid going last, as all eyes would be on me. So when the confident cookers who had gone first were distracted by a search for the missing saltshaker, I stepped up to the burner.

No one noticed my sewing machine legs as I mimicked Kelly's Zamboni technique.

So far, so good. The tiny piece of eggshell that slipped in with the rest of the egg goo went unnoticed.

The white whitened. I was halfway in. Time for the flip.

Unfortunately, the salt had been located. I couldn't shake the attention of my classmates.

With all eyes on the pan, heads dipped in unison as I wound up for the flick.

A bit too much wrist, perhaps, as it spun beyond 180. But I managed to land it within the pan, or at least most of it. After a failed jiggle, I rescued the bit that was dangling off the side with an amateurish finger nudge.

"Oooooohh, close one," someone whispered.

I returned the pan to the burner and stared into the sizzling edges, spacing out as I let go of an all-too-familiar worry.

"Oh, James, you like it really well done," Nicole prodded.

It stung. But it was also a welcome cue. I flopped my rubbery egg onto the plate and tossed on some salt.

Down the hatch it went.

Quickly.

It was no accident that the attention of my classmates was so inescapable. The egg flip is a tension-filled micro moment. We were mired in a tangle of anticipatory questions.

Tension had taken over the room—directing our gazes and controlling the rhythm of our breathing.

Heads turned.

Voices dropped.

What if—

the egg flips but then slides off the edge o f t h e p a n does land on the roof the egg the egg reaches the ceiling crack.

Tension Is Everywhere

When you look for it, you can find tension within nearly every piece of engaging media. There is tension within the split screen of a cable news debate, in which analysts argue over the latest political hobnob. There's tension throughout your social media, served on platters that are vying for dominance. There's tension in advertisements. Perhaps most importantly, there's tension in everyday life.

For tension to be activated, there must be stakes—someone must be on the verge of loss. Will the superhero die? Will Wakanda really be forever?

But a moment doesn't need life-or-death stakes for its tension to be captivating. Some of the most tension-filled moments in our lives have rather low stakes that seem high in the moment.

In Kelly's class, what was at stake was shame. None of us wanted to be the student who would let their egg flop to the ground. And we would all focus on the egg-flipper to see if they would become that person.

Tension, on its own, is just an ingredient. It's not meant to be consumed in isolation. And if you've ever spent ninety minutes scrolling through tension-filled video after tension-filled video, then you know that the experience can waste your time as easily as it can grab you.

The key to tension is to position it so that it will pull you into the very thing that you need to care about. But how do you make it transformative?

Tension in Whale Eyes

In *Whale Eyes*, my strategy was to put my family in the hot seat. They became the canvas on which the tension of my condition was presented. Rather than continuing to pretend that we didn't instinctually delete photographs in which my eyes pointed especially outward—I leaned into the awkwardness, asking them directly,

"Do my eyes make me uglier?"

They were suspended within the unspoken tension that I had been living with my entire life. Caught in the friction between the way I look and ideal beauty standards. It came alive in my older brother's response. His hesitation and body language are revealing. He is my brother, and he can't really say "yes," but he and viewers alike know that eyes like mine are not seen as conventionally attractive.

"I wouldn't say so," he eventually eked out.

But even his response—though polite and kind as Kirk always is—was revealing. *I* wouldn't say so. That still left room for others to disagree.

Each of these little questions is like its own egg flip. A micro moment in which I, as the question asker, held my breath, unsure how the egg would land. Unsure how the family member would answer.

These micro moments created an attention-grabbing frame within which I could finally explain my eyes. Perhaps that's the hidden superpower of tension—to create an opening in attention: a little void in which you can fit a precise story that creates understanding. Alone, the void is of little use. But if a kernel of understanding lingers within its boundaries, your audience may opt to grab on to it.

Transformation

In the final minutes of Kelly's class, I had an opening to deliver a kernel of understanding.

The kicker—the thing that makes her class an actual class instead of a hang-out-and-eat-with-your-friends— occurs in the final half hour. She gives you a prompt and ten minutes to handwrite a response.

When time is up, each person reads their response in front of the entire class. There's no wiggling out. No getting saved by the bell. No way to avoid the critique and exposé of self.

The shared reading, and the shared roughness, create a bond.

We grabbed pencils and pens and unlined sheets of paper. And with Kelly's cue, began turning scrambled thoughts into legible sentences.

As I recalled the anxiety of the egg flip, I wasn't thinking about the tension or analysis of storytelling techniques. Instead, I was thinking about holding that pan with all those eyes fixated on me, and watching with uncertainty as the egg turned over on itself. The experience brought me to a place that was familiar.

I knew this tense grip on the handle. The split second of insecurity when I didn't really know where this thing that was flying right in front of me really was—unsure if I was going to make contact when it came back down. I knew this fear of missing in front of a group of my peers, who would have no idea how I managed to whiff.

It brought me back to a time when I would take a deep breath and swing. A time when I was practicing hope.

As the clock ticked and classmates furiously scribbled their thoughts on the page, I did something I had never done before. For the first time in my life, I wrote—honestly and unflinchingly—about my eyes.

I wrote about what it meant to be standing there in my blue jersey, second to last in the lineup, still sharing that first-grade dream of becoming a major-league baseball player. I wrote about the awkward silence that follows a T-ball strikeout. About failing in front of teammates and parents, who were utterly puzzled as to why I couldn't hit the darn ball.

When it was my turn to read the words that I had furiously scribbled, I was so accustomed to sharing tension-busting sarcasm that I braced for laughter.

But there weren't any jokes. Instead, my voice read raw revelations, surprising me when it quivered. It was as if I was losing my voice precisely at the moment when I was finding it.

I began to feel the weight of something that I had been

holding in for so long finally ease up. For the first time,
I was surrounded by peers who were on the precipice of
understanding.

As I looked around after finishing, my throat still
starchy from the quivering, all I could think to myself,
over and over, was a promise I had made at the beginning
of class:

You will not be the second student to cry during this activity.

Use the Form

In 2018, a trend took root on Instagram: the film filter. From beaches to trips downtown to concerts with friends, everyone was making their photographs look as if they were taken on a film camera from the 1970s. We just couldn't get enough of it.

"It looks cool."

"It's a vibe."

"Whoaaa."

"Nice aesthetic."

Here's the thing. There's nothing wrong with the film filter itself. It's fun. It is a cool aesthetic.

But most of the time when you encounter it online, there's no actual reason for its use. When it comes to creating work that gets people to care, work that speaks to a wide audience, the form that you use—the structure of your sentences or the lens on your camera—are all choices. And they're choices that can help make your work stronger.

While most people using the film filter on social media had no motivation behind its use, I did encounter one person who used it strategically.

Alexandria Ocasio-Cortez picked up on the trend in a campaign ad before her election. Through her use of the film filter, she was subtly communicating with young voters, implying, *I speak your language visually, and I will speak your language in Congress.* Without using words, she was advertising that she was in touch with—and could advocate for—youth in an otherwise geriatric Congress.

Now, you might be thinking, *Who cares?* But there is an important point here: The form you use to tell a story can secretly push its message forward. You can use your form to underscore your thesis and sharpen its impact. Learning the rules of that form—and how to meaningfully break them—is key.

Sight Un-Scene

In *Whale Eyes*, my approach was to take advantage of the medium of film to simulate the way that I see. I hijack your vision and allow you to see through my eyes, so you can live for a few minutes in a world that is constantly jumping.

But I also played with form to accentuate what it means to be seen. The traditional documentary interview involves a person sitting to the left or right of the frame and looking across centerline. You leave some room on the side where they are looking. That's called the look space.

But I abandoned this. And instead, I had my family look directly into the camera's lens. I did the same when I turned the camera on myself. This positioning accentuated my difference. It's the angle at which my eye misalignment is the most glaring. But it also played into the thesis of the film. This is a film about eye contact.

And it is through the language of film that I give you, the viewer, the time and space to look into my eyes without having to feel awkward about it.

Because I am in front of your face virtually, rather than literally, you can actively practice looking into my eyes. It is as if—through the form of video—I am sending you a postcard that says,

Go ahead,
    please stare.

Invert the Narrative

"Could you make one for stuttering?"

I had received the video request numerous times. And I sensed a parallel with those who had reached out to me. The dominant societal narrative surrounding stuttering focuses on overcoming a stutter. Defeating it. Victory.

But 20 percent of those who stutter as children will continue doing so into adulthood. This particular sector of the stuttering community was drawn to the acceptance of Whale Eyes. But could the same be done for their condition?

I will admit, I was wary at first.

Film is all about pacing. And online video moves particularly quickly. The timing and delivery of each word must be maximized to prevail in the battle against the viewer's attention span.

I wasn't sure how to make disfluent speech hold its own. But, as is often the case in creative work, the stumbling block unveiled an essential opportunity. I began to ask what would happen if we flipped the narrative around this idea of overcoming.

I reached out to John Hendrickson, a journalist at *The Atlantic*. John developed a severe stutter at age four. Despite years of intensive interventions, nothing seemed to work, and he continues to stutter to this day.

John and I connected over our commonalities. We are both journalists. We each made pieces about our own conditions, both of which evolved into memoirs. John's feature in *The Atlantic* about Joe Biden's stutter, as well as his own, went viral after its release. We each knew what it meant to have a part of our being suddenly launched into the public sphere as we became overnight spokespeople for conditions that we, ourselves, were still processing.

It might appear that John was particularly ill-suited for an online short doc. But what if this form, which had previously excluded people like John, could actually help us all become more comfortable listening to those who stutter? What if it could turn out-trigue into understanding? What if the tension of this moment could push us to become better listeners?

Doing so would require an inversion of the narrative around stuttering. I would have to approach this not as an issue with speech but rather—an issue with listening.

A few years earlier, John had been interviewed in a PBS documentary about Joe Biden. I downloaded the interview from YouTube and began an experiment. What would it sound like if I took out his stutter entirely? On the one hand, this made me uncomfortable. It would be as if someone downloaded a photograph of me and photoshopped my eyes so that they were perfectly aligned. I was taking apart a piece of him. But, as a purely personal experiment, I decided to give it a try.

I spent a few minutes editing out every stutter: every block and every repetition. Then I played back the clip. John was fluent. Or at least, he sounded fluent.

I felt something change within me. Nothing John said had changed. I kept in every word. But my relationship with his words had shifted. My judgment of John, himself, had changed. I hadn't realized that John is extraordinarily eloquent. In typical on-camera interviews, many subjects meander halfway down the block and back before they reach a conclusion.

John landed each sentence on point. I simply hadn't trained my ear to become comfortable with the cadence of a stutter. Simply put, I was experiencing out-trigue. And I was finding that the form of video could be a powerful tool to confront this sensation.

Not a tool for John, as viewers might initially assume, but instead, the reverse—a tool for helping all of us become better listeners.

Machinations

I traveled to New York and interviewed John at the *Times'* film studio. It was a drastic upgrade from the squeaky-stool-in-a-bedroom *Whale Eyes* setup. Rather than shouting down the laundry chute for the rest of my family to quiet down because we were filming, I used the *Times'* more sophisticated solution—a little red "On Air" light.

There was luxury in having a second and third pair of hands to assist in the filming.

I interviewed John for three hours, pummeling him with questions. I then asked him to call local restaurants and automated customer service lines, filming his response as he was interrupted—or as those on the other end of the line grew confused.

Over the next few months, as I edited John's words into a story arc, I dreamed of a machine that would simulate what I had experienced when playing with John's earlier interview. One that would allow viewers to appreciate his extraordinary eloquence while catching themselves in the act of misjudging.

Admittedly, the idea was "out there" and risky. But if I could use a device that would take out all of John's stutters and then slowly add them back in, it might push the viewer to actively build their tolerance for stuttering as they watched.

I was walking a tightrope. If poorly executed, it could teeter toward becoming offensive. So I carefully sifted through the interview, one sound bite at a time. I knew if I could get the audience inside John's head, we could build empathy, and with that empathy would come increased patience. But I still needed a justification—a reason why the machine would suddenly start letting in more of his stutters—that wouldn't feel forced or infantilizing.

I experimented with different "levels" like an arcade game, speeds like a highway, and "gears" like a car.

The breakthrough came when I began sorting out the different types of stutters. I realized I could add in one type of stutter at a time. First leaving in his repetitions, then his prolongations, and finally, his blocks. John could describe each type of stutter as it was added into his speech pattern. This would enable him to provide a guided tour to an increasingly patient audience.

I was excited by the idea, but when I pitched it to the *Times* and shared a draft, the reviews were mixed. It didn't help that this machine I was envisioning didn't yet exist, leaving much of the film filled with blank frames and titles that read "Insert machine here."

At one point, it was suggested that I think about dropping the piece entirely. There was an idea there, but it didn't seem to be functioning. Throughout the series, the *Times* had given me a nearly infinite creative leash, and it appeared that I had become hopelessly entangled in it.

Instead of giving up, I went to eBay. I needed to make this device, and I believed that with a visual, the metaphor would be something that viewers would buy into. Initially, I had envisioned a cardboard contraption with wires sticking out of it and a Styrofoam cup that John would speak into. I had wanted to inject some levity into the piece—and make clear to the audience that this was an imagined device.

But for the audience to buy into the concept, I now realized that I needed a machine that was substantial and convincing. It would need three levers—one to remove each type of stutter. I scoured the web for vintage machinery: old telephones, fax machines, antiquated kitchen devices. I needed something that clicked and felt mechanical— delicate yet intricate. I finally stumbled on a Paymaster check-writing machine from the 1960s. It's a squat little machine, light green, with chrome accents, and this one was in near pristine condition. It had eight nubbins that you could slide up and down, and a huge lever on the side.

Sixty dollars later, the machine arrived. It was heavy: Nearly half the cost was shipping.

I began making alterations. I disguised the eight mini-levers as three large ones, and then I printed labels for "Blocks," "Prolongations," and "Repetitions" on metallic paper.

I removed the large handle and flipped the machine around, turning the back of the Paymaster, with its printed mesh design, into the front of what I was beginning to call the Listen-O-Meter. The mesh pattern provided a "screen" onto which I would digitally project John's face. And then, using YouTube tutorials and animation software, I stuck John inside.

Speed Bumps

When I sent the next draft to the *Times*, they had a change in faith—the concept was working. But the Listen-O-Meter looked a bit scrappy.

It needed an upgrade. So I did what you do when your hands are sticky with glue, your floor is littered with scraps of metal, your scissors are too dull, and you're still not quite satisfied with the result: I called my brother.

I lucked out on timing. One of Kirk's designs had just been scrapped because of supply chain issues, leaving him with a burning desire to accomplish something. So he drove up from Irvine ready to strip-mall. We hit Staples. And Michaels. Save for the five minutes spent looking at model cars, we moved fast. We affixed metal plates to levers. Stickers to metal. And hot glue to tape.

A few hours into his visit, the Listen-O-Meter was becoming real.

The purpose of the Listen-O-Meter was to slow down. To break the high-speed, attention-grabbing standard of online video. To come to peace with the pauses. And to fill in the gaps in John's speech with our own patience. The response was overwhelming.

Aside from the interview, the video was made on a minimal budget, partly in New York, yes, but mostly in the confines of my bedroom, with my mattress folded up against the window to block the sun, as I sat in the same spot where I had filmed much of *Whale Eyes*.

In a sea of big-budget documentaries and large-scale news operations, a video like this one is a tiny lifeboat. But the tiny boats are nimble and flexible, creative and free. It's not the cost of the camera, but the vision of the person wielding it, that is ultimately most important. And that vision is yours.

Dear Reader,

Give me something precise to care about.
Capture my attention with tension. Make
me lean into out-trigue. Use the form to
transform my understanding. And flip
the narrative.

I want to be moved by your story.
And I want to care.

Flying Weather

When I was six years old, my mother sat me down, looked me in the eye, and told me she could fly.

Perhaps that's not surprising. Anyone can fly. Commercial flying is a feat of human ingenuity, and at any one moment there are, on average, half a million people in the sky.

But my mom wasn't talking about metal tubes. In fact, she hates airplanes. She has an irrational fear of them. On the few flights she takes per year, she spends taxi, takeoff, and times of turbulence vigorously factoring polynomials to ease her airplane anxiety.

You might think, then, that she meant flying in the metaphorical sense. Parents all over the world tell their kids that they can do great things, that they will achieve success—even suggesting that their kids will "take flight" and "soar."

But what my mom described wasn't the type of flying that we associate with dreams that have come true. When Mom spoke of flying, it was not in the future tense. When she spoke of flying, it wasn't metaphorical.

She told us that she had literally flown. That she had spread her arms, and leaned into the wind, and her feet had lifted off the ground. She told us she had flown on multiple occasions, and that she had once touched the upper branches of a pine tree.

And as we stared in disbelief and questioned her every detail, she would tell us how she flew.

The conditions had to be just right. You had to wait for "flying weather." And you would know that it was flying weather because it would be windy. There would be gusts so strong that it would be difficult to walk in a straight line. A greenish haze would tinge the sky, and the air would be balmy—sweet and alive with an earthy, tropical freshness.

She told us that during "flying weather," the branches of the giant hemlocks in front of her childhood home engaged in a dance that was as gargantuan as it was graceful. They swayed to impossible angles as they were driven downward, only to catch another gale-force crest and rise again.

When she was a child, her flights were minimal. She would be lifted a few inches, and deposited perhaps a foot or two to either side, catching herself in a deep knee bend as she scrambled for balance. I wondered if she had set it off with a jump.

But each time my brother and I rolled our eyes or told her that she was tricking us and that we didn't believe her, she would only smile and say,

"Well, maybe one day, you will fly too."

Skepticism

I imagine you are feeling a bit of out-trigue by now. Even when I tell this story to close friends or confidants, I can feel a void growing between us.

Friends take on the stance of starers—eyes narrowing and arms crossed. I can practically hear the question bouncing in their brain: "What's wrong with you?"

But in these moments, I felt no urge to ask them the same.

I understood their skepticism. And I understand yours, too. Taking flight without wings sounds more like a fantastical idea than a fantastic one. Certainly, the Wright brothers could have saved time if they had just spread their arms.

But no matter how much I try to level my head, or skept my -cism, I can't let go of the small possibility that perhaps there is truth to this claim. Maybe she really did lift her arms and feel her feet leave the ground as she was pushed by the wind.

Maybe she is telling the truth.

Opti-cism

There are a few reasons I think my mother may have actually flown.

First and foremost, Mom is a terrible liar. And she's quick to dissolve any lies, particularly when they involve fooling her children. My faith in the tooth fairy didn't make it past six.

Second, her claim was not egoic. Her description of flight couldn't be further from the motivational, your-future-will-be-bright, catapult-toward-the-stars-even-if-there's-no-oxygen-out-there platitudes of a graduation ceremony. She never tried to sell us on the idea that flying was some majestic accomplishment. That life up there was any better than life down here.

If anything, her description of flying was a warning. She described being pushed and pulled by each gust, losing control, experiencing a visceral fear. She was entirely overcome by the power of the winds.

Her experience of flying wasn't a seamless ascension into the ether, but a surrender to the elements that gave her lift. A surrender that was humbling.

"Are you sure you're not making that up?" we would ask.

But she never relented. And still she declares—always with a mischievous smile—that it's true.

What If

Even if you're drowning in cringe, or overcome by out-trigue, I want you to put those emotions aside for a second.

Just imagine—for a few paragraphs—that flying is possible.

be   like   fly?
        it   to

    would

What

                                        it?
                                about
                            go
                you   even
        would
How

For starters, if you want to fly, you have to believe that flying is possible. You have to be completely unfazed by an idea that many think is absurd and unrealistic. You can't allow social pressures to keep you inside. You have to be willing to take a calculated risk.

If you want to fly, you have to pay attention to the weather. And you have to be willing to go outside when it is windy. You can't be put off by people who tell you that flying is only possible in a metal tube. You have to be willing to run for the door with the excitement of a child the minute you sense hints of "flying weather."

As you take your first step outside, you realize that the wind is much stronger than you thought possible. You feel self-conscious and unsteady, as if you're going to be torn off the ground. But if you want to fly, you have to be willing to let go. You have to let go of the safety and security that is standing on the ground. And you have to let go of all the things that you thought flying would be.

Most of us imagine flying as a moment—the moment when we're above the ground with our arms spread out, looking at the land and trees below. But perhaps it is a far more sensory experience than could ever be conjured by the human imagination. Either way, it begins in struggle—a struggle to work with and against the elements.

As you stumble across the field, allowing yourself to be pushed and pulled by the gusts, you're suddenly not sure that you will make it off the ground. But that's okay. Because if you want to fly, you have to be willing to surrender yourself to the weather.

Maybe you will spread your arms and feel a breeze, but your feet never leave the soft embrace of the grass. Or perhaps you will take flight—maybe just for a minute—but with no one else there to witness, you will return to your family with glee, only for them to dismiss your tale as fallacy.

As the sharp breath of air swishes past and you feel it stinging your cheeks and pushing against your hands, the ground suddenly becomes lighter. And then you, too, begin to feel lighter. In this moment of triumph and joy and confusion, you will realize that you have absolutely no idea how to fly. But if you want to fly, you have to be willing to learn from your mistakes. There is no manual. There are no checklists, and there is no answer key in the back of the book. You must trust your own ability to gain lift, to steer skillfully, and to lower yourself gently. You have to be willing to teach yourself. To learn within your limits.

The truth about flying is that it's not a singular journey with a predetermined location. You cannot force yourself on the wind—you must release yourself to it. It's an unpredictable series of tugs and lurches. And it's only when you are willing to embrace the loss of balance that you will begin to feel the exhilaration that is flying.

Each Time I Fly

Perhaps it comes as no surprise that each time I spread my arms and breathe in the sweet tropical winds, I have stayed rooted firmly on the ground. The truth is, there is only one person under the sky who will ever know if my mom took flight. For the rest of us, she has left a small bead of possibility in a vast ocean of doubt.

But even when we were fifteen and seventeen, as the wind picked up, Kirk and I would hear a gleeful yell from downstairs, "Hey, boys, it's flying weather!" And every time without fail—even late at night—we would race outside, feel the breeze, and spread our arms. We would taste the air and try to surrender to the conditions, telling ourselves that on this day, that this time, that in this weather, we, too, could fly.

As we staggered in the wind, we would each develop our own strategy for flying.

Kirk would study the direction of the gusts—finding patches of raucous air that were unblocked by the house and undissolved by trees.

Reed—youngest by far—often resorted to running, sometimes in circles, often without much care for which way the wind was blowing. He added in little skips. As if he were a plane taking off.

Mom leaned backward into the wind, sometimes with her jacket spread, testing her weight against its force.

I would twist my arms up and down as if they were the flaps of an airplane—hoping it might have some impact on my aerodynamism. And then, after a few failed attempts, I would see if I could cheat, stretching on my tippy-toes and jumping forward as a gust approached.

Even the family pragmatist, Dad, who has spent much of his life keeping his lofty family grounded in reality, has been caught spreading out his arms in a gust or two.

After fifteen minutes of being pushed and pulled by the wind but never lifted, our resolution would dissolve into laughter. Laughter at the absurdity of our bodily positions and our attempts to surrender to high winds. Laughter at the fact that we could barely make out each other's words as we tried to yell louder than the rustling of the tree branches.

Eventually, as the wind died down, or the conditions became dangerous and the family pragmatist spoke up, we began to let go of the idea that today was the day we would fly.

As we walked back inside, we pestered Mom with questions.

"When you flew, was it like this or windier?"

"It was warmer, right?"

"Did the sky have more glow to it?"

She always provided a diagnosis as to why today wasn't quite flying weather, but she made sure to affirm that we were, indeed, so close.

"The air isn't quite sweet enough."

"Not quite enough tang."

"The sky was a bit more green."

As we walked back inside, wondering if she had been hurled by a hurricane or tossed by a tornado, we weren't so much defeated as we were curious.

-Trigued.

Exuberant.

As if for a few seconds, we had really, truly lived.

Whether

Flying weather was never really about the whether. It was never about whether a series of freak wind events occurred off the coast of Maine in the summers of 1972, '83, and '85. It was never about whether that wind was powerful enough to propel a person into the air for more than a few seconds. It was never about whether my mom had actually flown.

Flying weather is about what wires us into caring and believing.

To this day, despite skepticism and disbelief, I instinctually run outside on a warm and windy day when the weather might be just right for flying.

To this day, I know that if I call out, "It's flying weather!" Kirk will emerge from his engineering problem, and Dad from behind his computer, and Mom from her studio where she is coaching someone out of some sort of problem, and Reed will pop out from wherever it is that Reed goes. Together we will venture outside.

There is a reason that we stretch out our arms and attempt to surrender to the wind.

With her story, Mom pushed us into caring.

Through her out-trigue, tension, and this shared, precise moment, she made us forget everything else as we focused on the elements before us: The direction of the wind. The color of the sky. Our position in the grass. She made us care about the hints of green. The stiff thickness of the humidity. And the texture of the invisible energy that flowed between our fingers. She allowed us to experience firsthand what it means to place our trust in a force that is as wild and unpredictable as it is real.

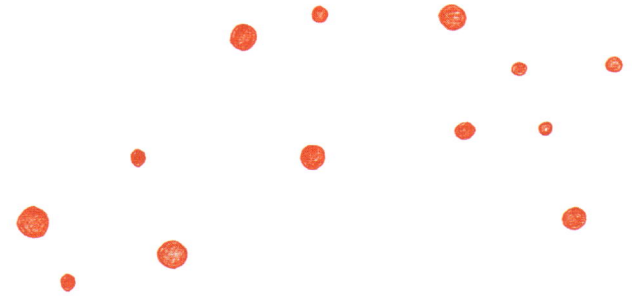

Flying weather is a form of communication. And even if we couldn't hear each other over the roaring winds, we were engaging in a silent communion. It's the same communion that I encountered when neighbors suddenly began looking back into the eye that was looking at them. They weren't just saying, *I watched your film*; they were silently declaring, *I want our connection to be seamless.* It's the same communion that occurs when we take the time to listen to someone who stutters. We aren't just saying, *I'm aware of the proper etiquette*; rather, we send a strong and powerful message: *Your words matter.* It's the same type of communion that takes place when we run into Paul at the grocery store and take the time to remind him who we are. In that moment, we don't just share the relief of finally recognizing someone, but the joy of truly knowing them.

In this form of communication, the meaning within each message is amplified—factorialized by the care that is within.

As my family stood side by side, through bouts of laughter and with wind-dried eyes, we weren't just testing our ability to fly; we were sending each other a message:

I will surrender to the wind with you.

Even in your loftiest and most absurd dreams,
when I'm not even sure if I believe you,
I will still believe in *you.*

And I will ignore the confused stares of neighbors and
passersby as I try to find lift with you.

I will add my own spunk and develop my own
technique as I try to take flight with you.

And I will ask myself to believe for a second that
maybe today is the day when we will see each other fly.

In my family, we rarely say the phrase "I love you," because it feels both overly dramatic and shockingly shallow, but the message we send to each other by outstretching our arms and leaning into the wind has always felt like it held more meaning—and more care— than those three words ever could.

A Note on Surgery

Whale Eyes is meant to foster conversations around the social impacts of strabismus, as well as raise awareness of the experience of disability. It is not meant to be taken as medical advice.

With that said, I recognize that many readers are in the midst of complicated health care decisions. Each case is different, and requires the expertise of a doctor. For those in the US, ophthalmologists can be found here: aapos.org/find-a-doctor.

Although my personal story includes two instances of strabismus surgeries that did not pan out as hoped, I am part of a minority. Overwhelmingly, strabismus surgery is effective and safe.

The availability of new technologies to treat strabismus has changed within my lifetime. In my teenage years, I was cautioned by several doctors that my own rare complications put me at an elevated risk of permanent double vision. However, the increased availability of adjustable sutures allows doctors to fine-tune corrections after surgery, with some doctors having the ability to make adjustments even several days after surgery, significantly reducing that risk.

Even in cases when stereoscopic vision cannot be attained, strabismus surgery is not merely a cosmetic adjustment—it can have numerous medical benefits.

I'll make my choice about surgery in private. As you will make yours. But whichever choice we make, I do not believe that it undermines the importance of a broader conversation about the social impact of misaligned eyes.

In the wake of publishing *Whale Eyes* in the *New York Times*, I received countless messages from fellow strabismus patients. It was abundantly clear—regardless of surgical outcome or medical history—that there were thousands of us, who yearned for the opportunity to discuss the social impact of our condition. The urgency of these messages led me to accept Penguin's request that I write this book. I have been humbled by the opportunity to foster this conversation, and I will continue to push for understanding, compassion, and accurate representation in media, so that we are better able to forge strong, human connections. Those interested in learning more about facial differences may find the following resources helpful:

moebiussyndrome.org

faceequalityinternational.org

Positiveexposure.org

Faceoutproject.com

Acknowledgments

Whale Eyes is about kindness, acceptance, and understanding. I am grateful that these values aren't just written on the page but were embedded into the process of its creation.

This book wouldn't exist were it not for my editor, Nick Magliato, who has supported this project as it evolved and found its form. It's an extraordinary privilege to get to write the book that you want to write. Especially when you want it to twist, fold, and be held upside down. I am grateful to Nick, Mary Claire Cruz, and the entire team at Penguin for their support of this vision.

Thanks to Brian Rea, a dream collaborator, whose genius and emotion infuse such joy into this work. When we first approached Brian, I wrote him a letter, in which

I noted that *at its core, this book is about the joy of turning out-trigue into connection. It's about finding moments when we are within the realm of someone's difference, and yet they feel that there is no part of their being that needs to be hidden, minimized, or ignored. When out-trigue dissolves, it gives way to a rare and special type of joy. I don't quite have a word for this yet. But it's a feeling I get when I look at your work.*

Thank you, Brian, for bringing this emotion to life through your illustrations.

Thanks to my agent, Stephen Barr, who has been beyond wonderful in welcoming me to the world of publishing, as well as Erica McGrath and the entire team at Writers House.

Thanks to the team at the *New York Times* Opinion Video: Adam B. Ellick, Jonah M. Kessel, Emily Holzknecht, and Andrew Blackwell.

The second half of this book is in many ways a love letter to the Center for Documentary Studies at Duke. It's the place where *Whale Eyes* was born and has long been my documentary North Star. Thanks to Kelly Alexander, Susie Post-Rust, Steve Milligan, and Michaela O'Brien. Many thanks to Wesley Hogan, the former director of the CDS, with whom I developed the idea of "out-trigue" and began writing in greater detail about my vision—essays that would lead me to create *Whale Eyes*. And finally, thanks to my longtime mentor, Chris Sims, in whose class I produced the first version of the film *Whale Eyes*.

Thank you to Rinchen Doma, who has had a hand in many of my films (just look for the green bracelet), and whose kindness and patience helped me talk my way through the book. Many thanks to Dr. David Hunter and Dr. Lara Ameen for their thoughtful suggestions.

Thank you to my family:

Nan, who lifts our spirits during our "Arms with Nan" (Readers—if you are able, workout with your grandmother over Zoom, it will be the best fifteen minutes of your day);

Kirk, who is the kindest—and most helpful—person I know,

Reed, who is... Has anybody seen Reed? Is he here? Did he go birding?

Dad, who keeps our family grounded and taught me the power of a quick wit,

And Mom. So much of this book emerged through an ongoing conversation between the two of us—one that started before I could talk and continues to this day. There is no one whose opinion of my work I hold in higher regard.

Finally, I want to acknowledge the community that made this project possible. *Whale Eyes* and countless works like it exist because of the tireless work of the disability community, whose members have fought to create space for disabled voices—in the classroom, in journalism, and in publishing. Repeatedly, this community has proven that disability stories are not just essential to our understanding of ourselves and our world, but also that they are commercially viable—stories for which readers and viewers yearn.

When disabled people are included in media production, which is to say—when they are accommodated, listened to, and given creative control— the quality, accuracy, and reach of our work inevitably increases.

I will never know many of the names of those who fought to create the space for a book like *Whale Eyes*. But their collective actions are the reason that this project can exist. To them I say: *Thank you. Our world is a better, kinder, and more just place because you are in it.*

Citations

Barry, S. R. (2009). *Fixing my gaze: A scientist's journey into seeing in three dimensions.* Basic Books.

Buffenn, A . N. (2021). The impact of strabismus on psychosocial health and quality of life: a systematic review. *Survey of Ophthalmology, 66*(6), 1051–1064. https://doi.org/10.1016/j.survophthal.2021.03.005

Dohlman, J. C., Hunter, D. G., & Heidary, G. (2022). The impact of strabismus on psychosocial equity. *Seminars in Ophthalmology, 38*(1), 52–56. https://doi.org/10.1080/08820538.2022.2152701

Kothari, M., & Joshi, V. (2014). The perceived personality traits of adults with digitally induced large angle strabismus and the impact of its correction. *Indian Journal of Ophthalmology, 62*(7), 773–776. DOI: 10.4103/0301-4738.138617

Kushner, B. J. (2011). The efficacy of strabismus surgery in adults: A review for primary care physicians. *Postgraduate Medical Journal*, 87(1026), 269–273. https://doi.org/10.1136/pgmj.2010.108670

Mojon-Azzi, S. M., & Mojon, D. S. (2007). Opinion of Headhunters about the Ability of Strabismic Subjects to Obtain Employment. *Ophthalmologica, 221*(6), 430–433. https://doi.org/10.1159/000107506

Mojon-Azzi, S. M., Kunz, A., & Mojon, D. S. (2011). Strabismus and discrimination in children: Are children with strabismus invited to fewer birthday parties? *British Journal of Ophthalmology, 95*(4). https://doi.org/10.1136/bjo.2010.185793

Paysse, E. A., Steele, E. A., McCreery, K. M., Wilhelmus, K. R., & Coats, D. K. (2001). Age of the emergence of negative attitudes toward strabismus. *Journal of the American Association for Pediatric Ophthalmology and Strabismus, 5*(6), 361–366. https://doi.org/10.1067/mpa.2001.119243

Uretmen, O., Egrilmez, S., Kose, S., Pamukçu, K., Akkin, C., & Palamar, M. (2003). Negative social bias against children with strabismus. *Acta Ophthalmologica Scandinavica, 81*(2), 138–142. https://doi.org/10.1034/j.1600-0420.2003.00024.x